Costume Quest:

INVASION OF THE CANDY SNATCHERS

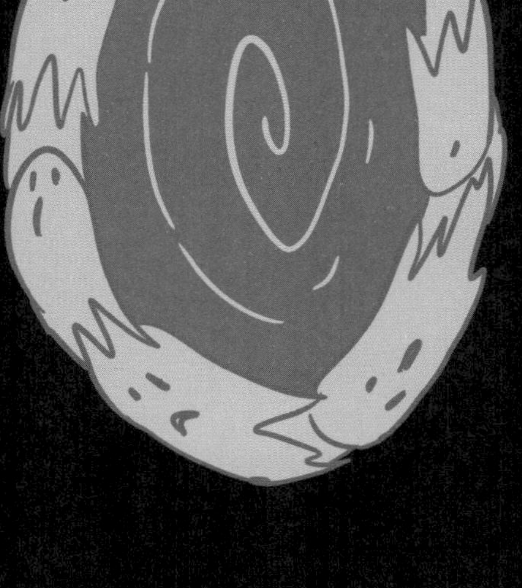

ONI PRESS

DOUBLE FINE

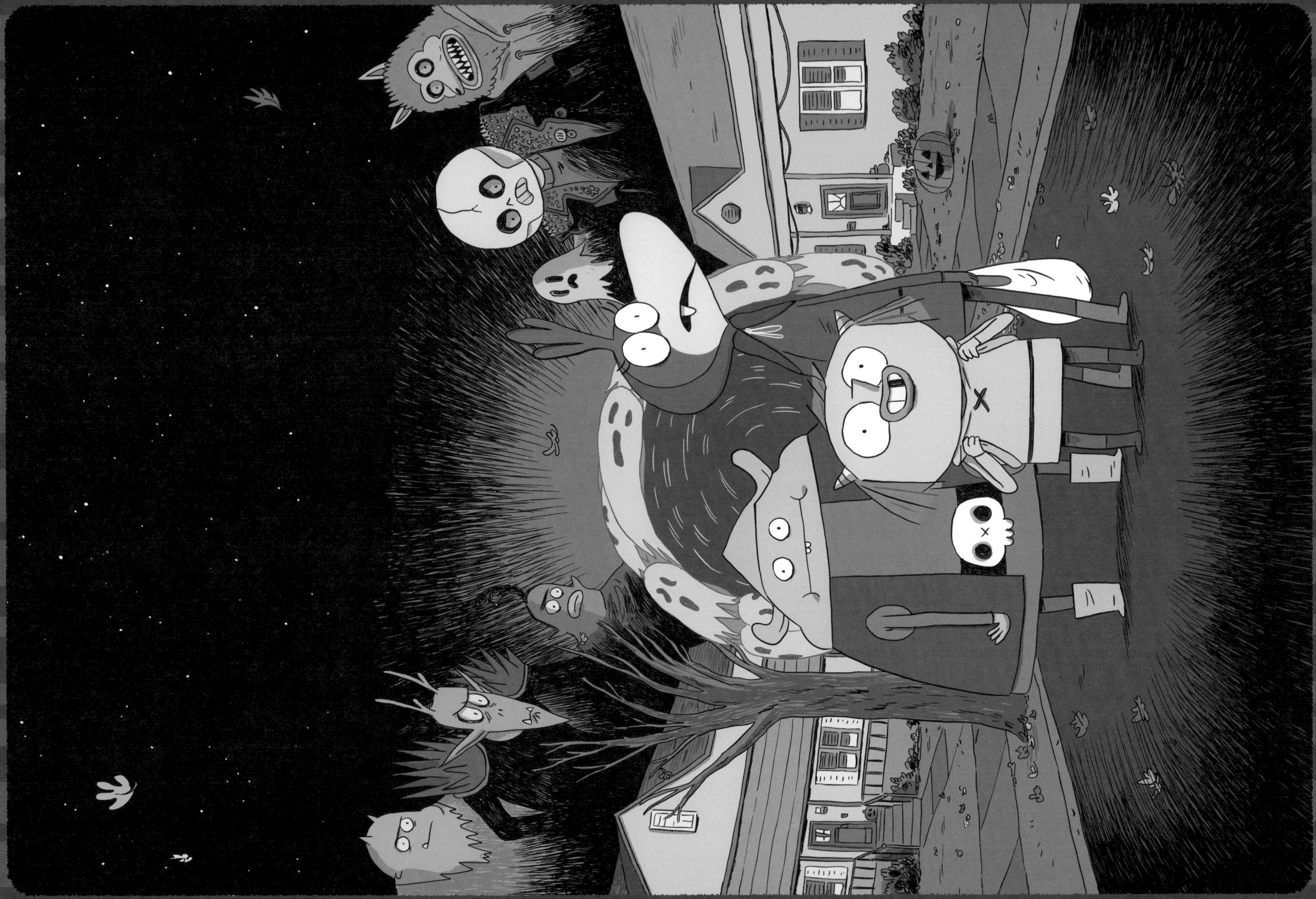

Costume Quest

INVASION OF THE CANDY SNATCHERS

By
Zac Gorman

Based on the Costume Quest world created by
Tasha Sounart and Double Fine Productions

Designed by
Keith Wood

Edited by
Charlie Chu

Published by Oni Press, Inc.

Joe Nozemack, publisher
James Lucas Jones, editor in chief
Tim Wiesch, VP of business development
Cheyenne Allott, director of sales
John Schork, director of publicity
Jason Storey, senior designer
Troy Look, production manager
Charlie Chu, editor
Robin Herrera, associate editor
Brad Rooks, inventory coordinator
Ari Yarwood, administrative assistant
Jung Lee, office assistant
Jared Jones, production assistant

Oni Press, Inc.

1305 SE Martin Luther King Jr. Blvd.

Suite A

Portland, OR 97214

USA

onipress.com • facebook.com/onipress • @onipress • onipress.tumblr.com

doublefine.com • @doublefine

magicalgametime.com • zacgorman.com • @zacgormania

First edition: October 2014

ISBN 978-1-62010-190-2
eISBN 978-1-62010-191-9

Library of Congress Control Number: 2014938500

10 9 8 7 6 5 4 3 2 1

PRINTED IN CHINA.

For my mom, for making my Halloween costumes, and my dad, for taking me to the comic store.

– Zac

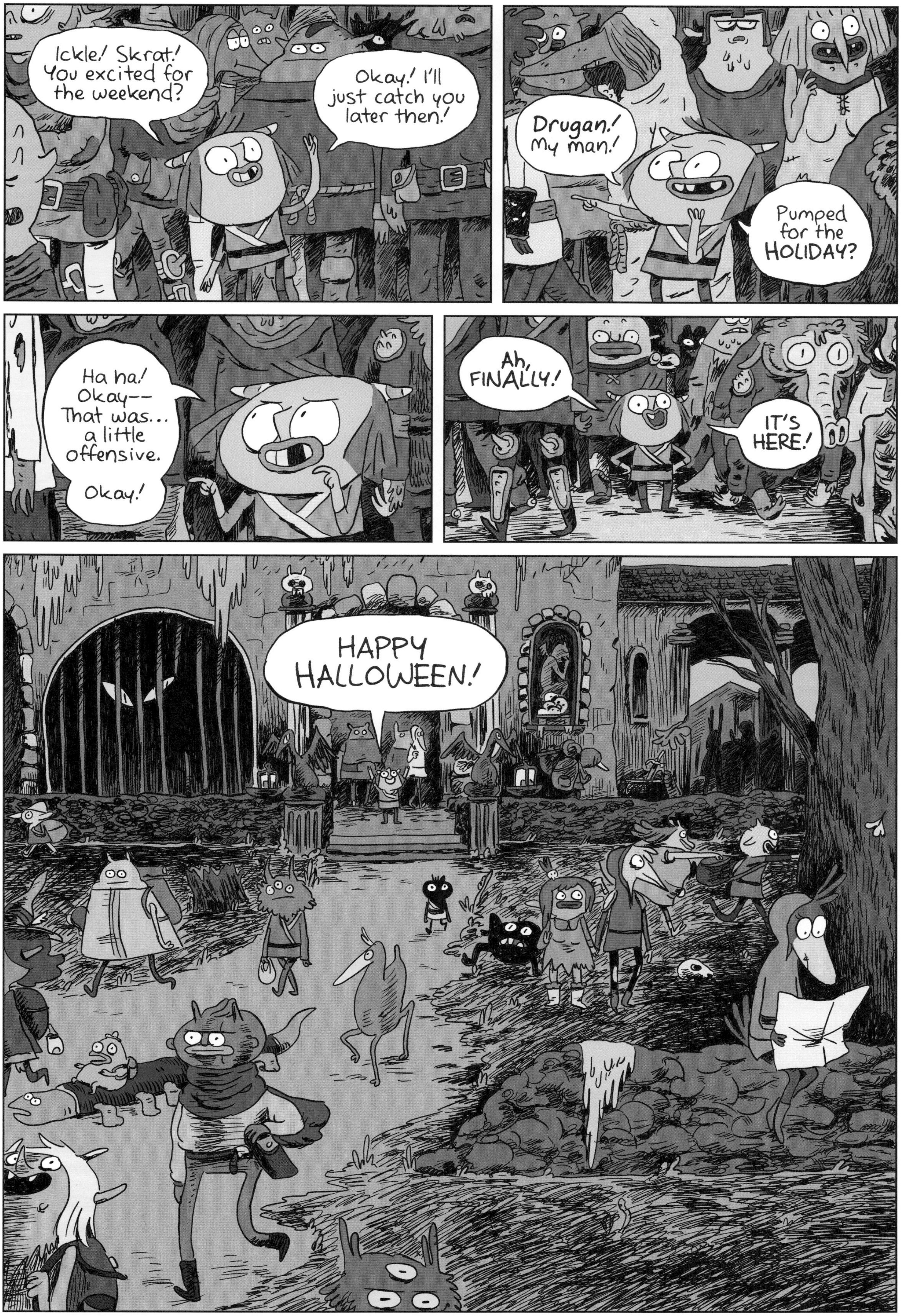
Ickle! Skrat! You excited for the weekend?
Okay! I'll just catch you later then!
Drugan! My man!
Pumped for the HOLIDAY?
Ha ha! Okay-- That was... a little offensive.
Okay!
Ah, FINALLY!
IT'S HERE!
HAPPY HALLOWEEN!

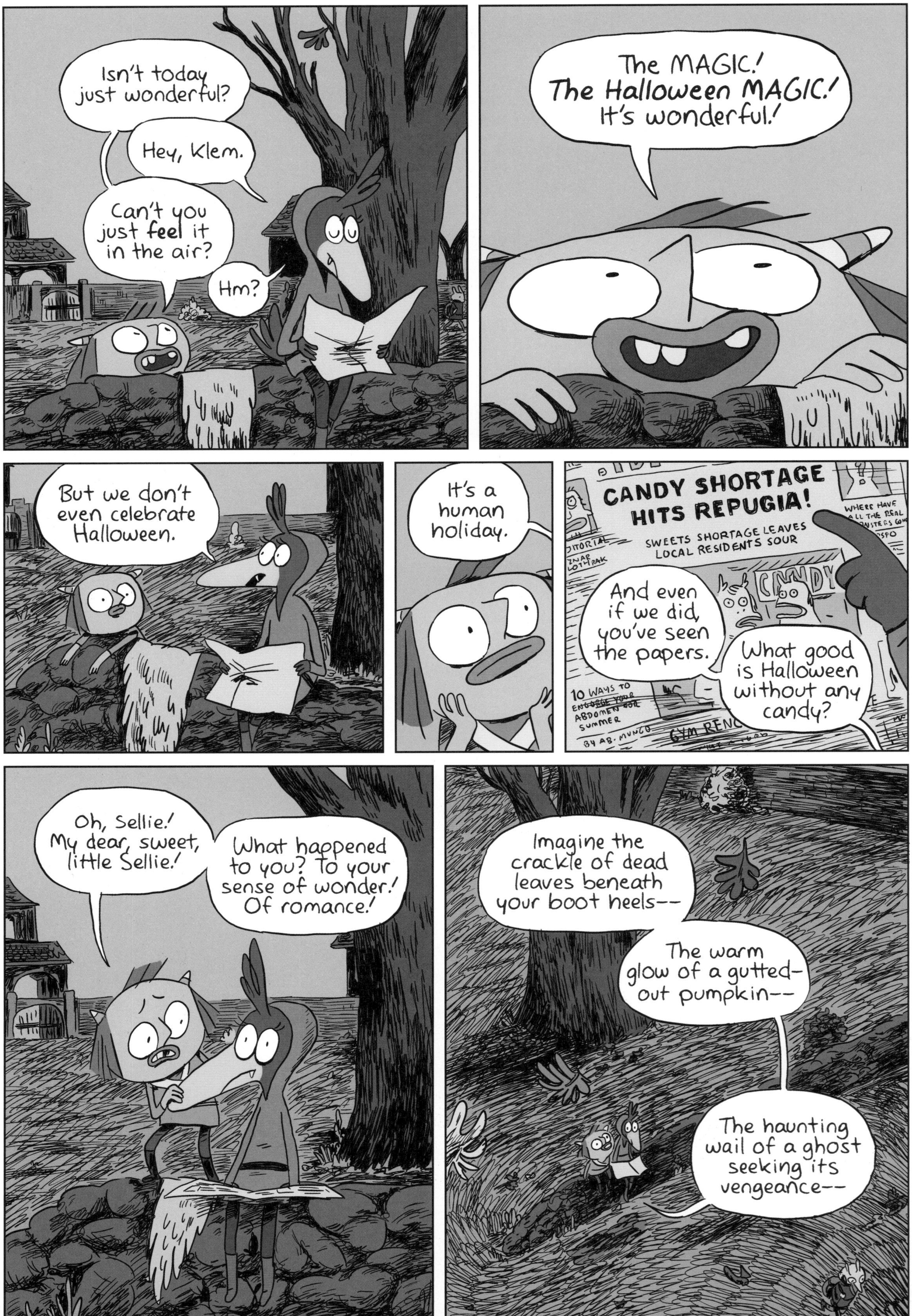
Isn't today just wonderful?
Hey, Klem.
Can't you just **feel** it in the air?
Hm?
The MAGIC! **The Halloween MAGIC!** It's wonderful!
But we don't even celebrate Halloween.
It's a human holiday.
CANDY SHORTAGE HITS REPUGIA!
SWEETS SHORTAGE LEAVES LOCAL RESIDENTS SOUR
And even if we did, you've seen the papers.
What good is Halloween without any candy?
Oh, Sellie! My dear, sweet, little Sellie!
What happened to you? To your sense of wonder! Of romance!
Imagine the crackle of dead leaves beneath your boot heels--
The warm glow of a gutted-out pumpkin--
The haunting wail of a ghost seeking its vengeance--

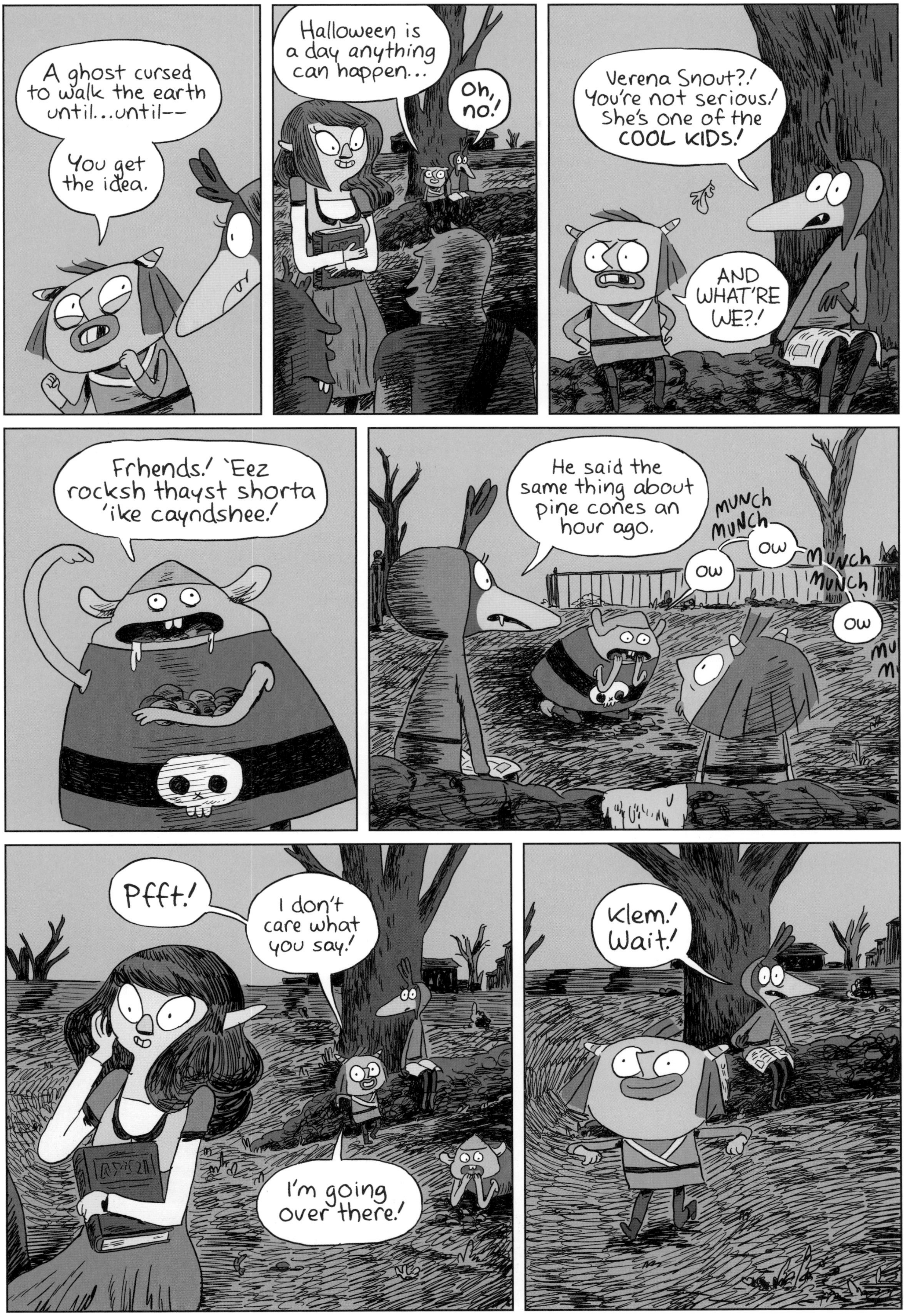
A ghost cursed to walk the earth until...until--
You get the idea.
Halloween is a day anything can happen...
Oh, no!
Verena Snout?! You're not serious! She's one of the COOL KIDS!
AND WHAT'RE WE?!
Frhends! 'Eez rocksh thayst shorta 'ike cayndshee!
He said the same thing about pine cones an hour ago.
MUNCH MUNCH
OW
OW
MUNCH MUNCH
OW
Pfft!
I don't care what you say!
I'm going over there!
Klem! Wait!

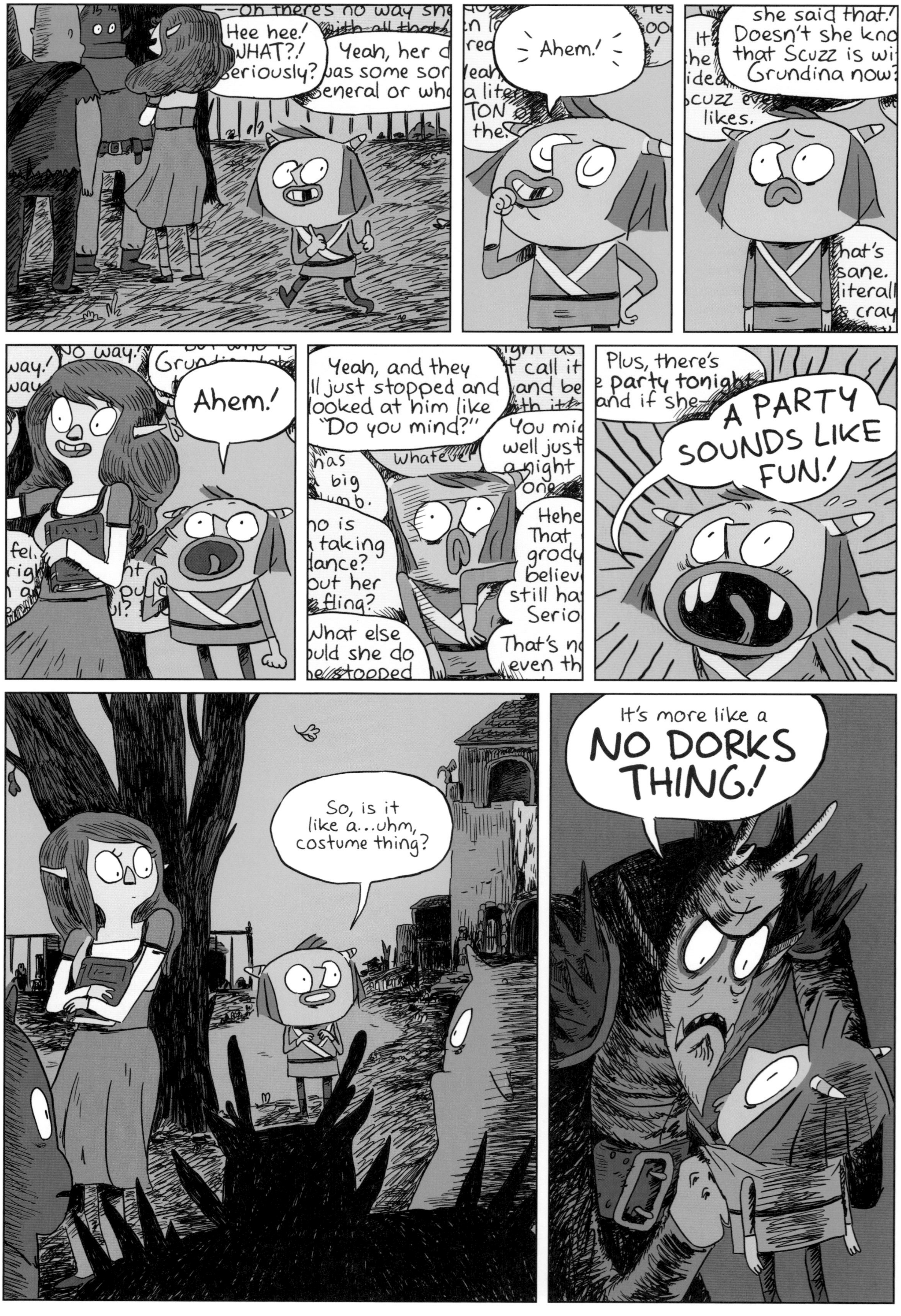
Ahem!
Ahem!
A PARTY SOUNDS LIKE FUN!
So, is it like a...uhm, costume thing?
It's more like a NO DORKS THING!

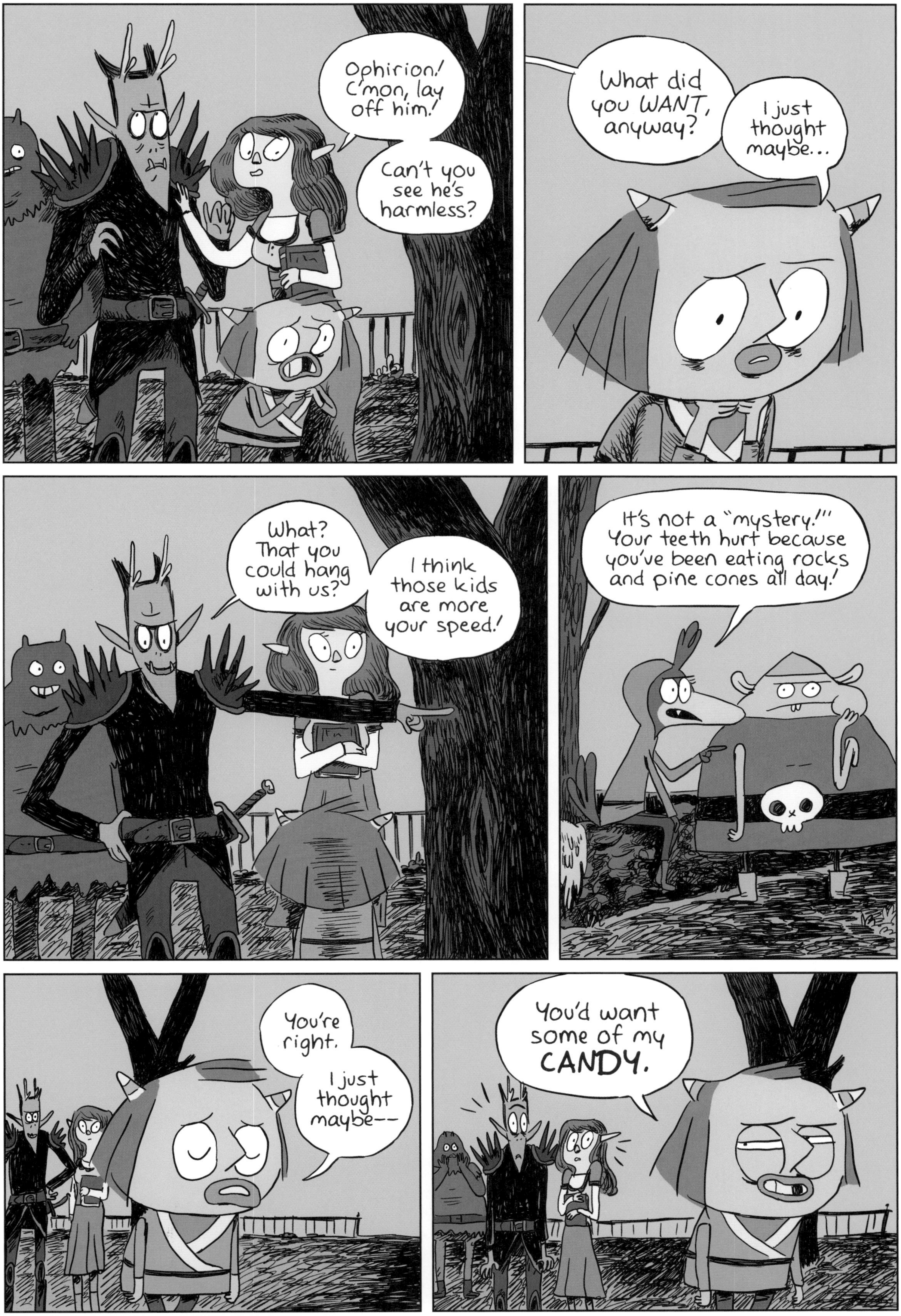
Ophirion! C'mon, lay off him!
Can't you see he's harmless?
What did you WANT, anyway?
I just thought maybe...
What? That you could hang with us?
I think those kids are more your speed!
It's not a "mystery!" Your teeth hurt because you've been eating rocks and pine cones all day!
You're right.
I just thought maybe--
You'd want some of my CANDY.

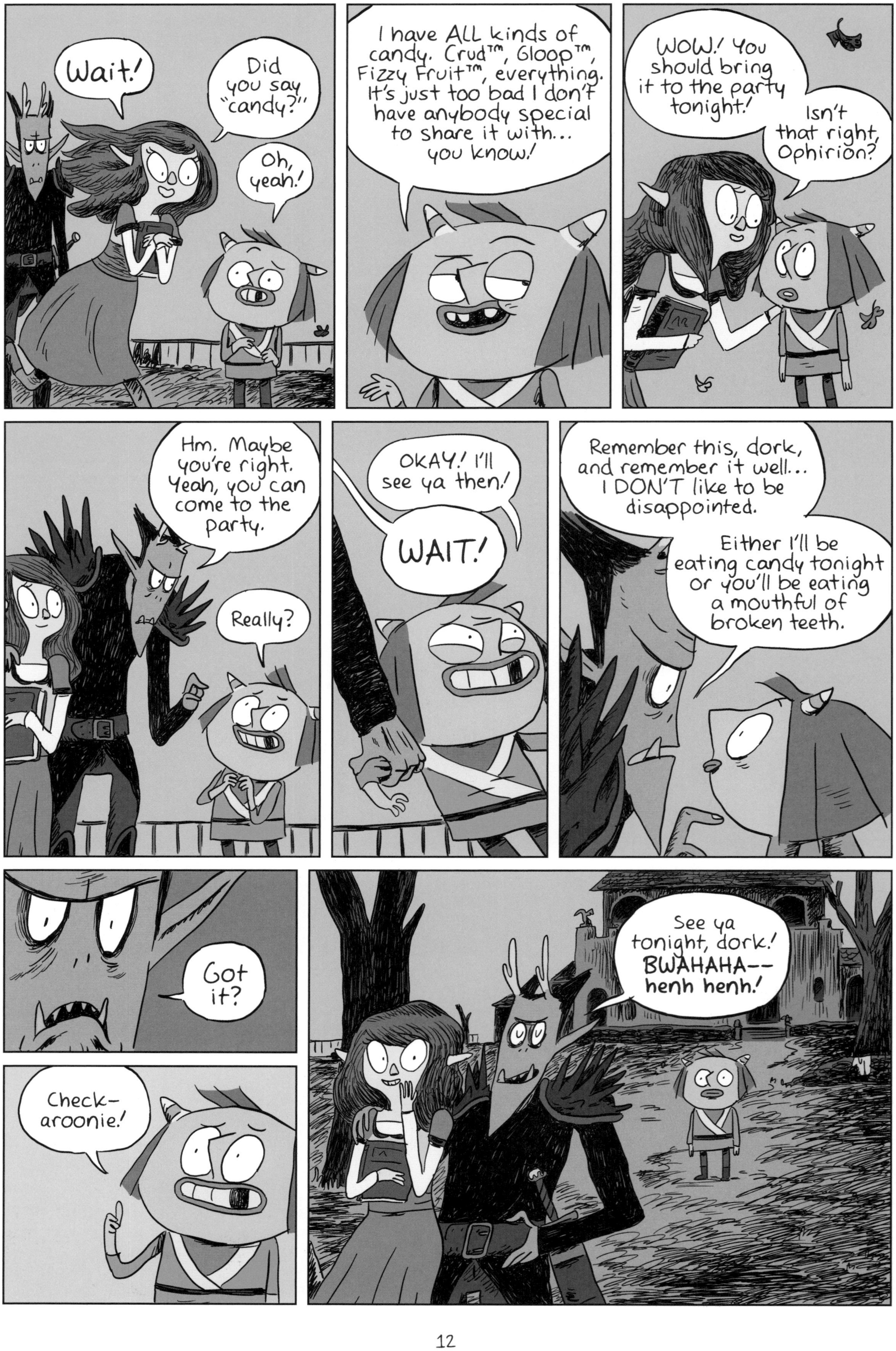
Wait!
Did you say "candy?"
Oh, yeah!
I have ALL kinds of candy. Crud™, Gloop™, Fizzy Fruit™, everything. It's just too bad I don't have anybody special to share it with... you know!
WOW! You should bring it to the party tonight!
Isn't that right, Ophirion?
Hm. Maybe you're right. Yeah, you can come to the party.
Really?
OKAY! I'll see ya then!
WAIT!
Remember this, dork, and remember it well... I DON'T like to be disappointed.
Either I'll be eating candy tonight or you'll be eating a mouthful of broken teeth.
Got it?
Check-aroonie!
See ya tonight, dork! BWAHAHA-- henh henh!

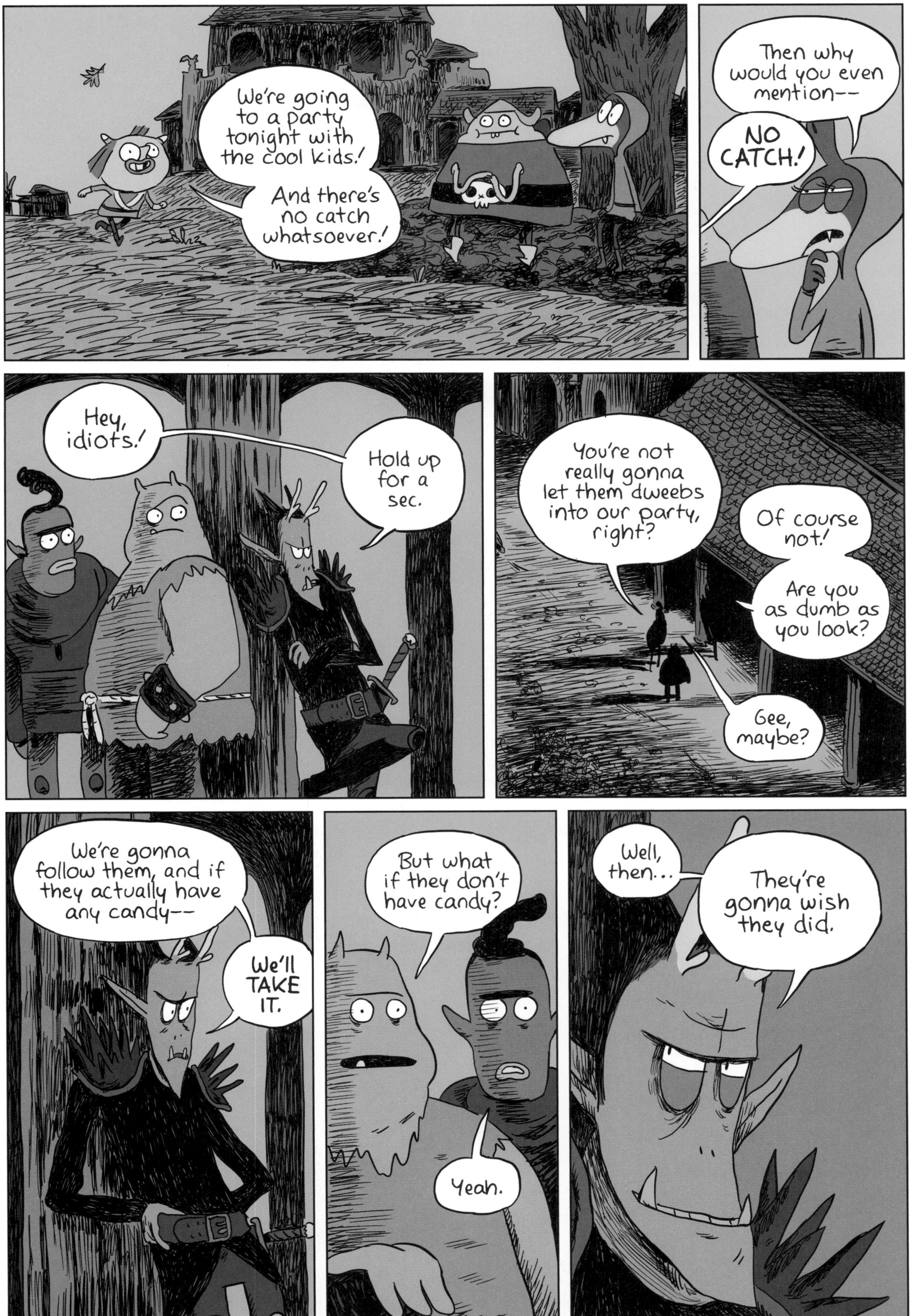
We're going to a party tonight with the cool kids.!
And there's no catch whatsoever.!
Then why would you even mention--
NO CATCH.!
Hey, idiots.!
Hold up for a sec.
You're not really gonna let them dweebs into our party, right?
Of course not.!
Are you as dumb as you look?
Gee, maybe?
We're gonna follow them, and if they actually have any candy--
We'll TAKE IT.
But what if they don't have candy?
Yeah.
Well, then...
They're gonna wish they did.

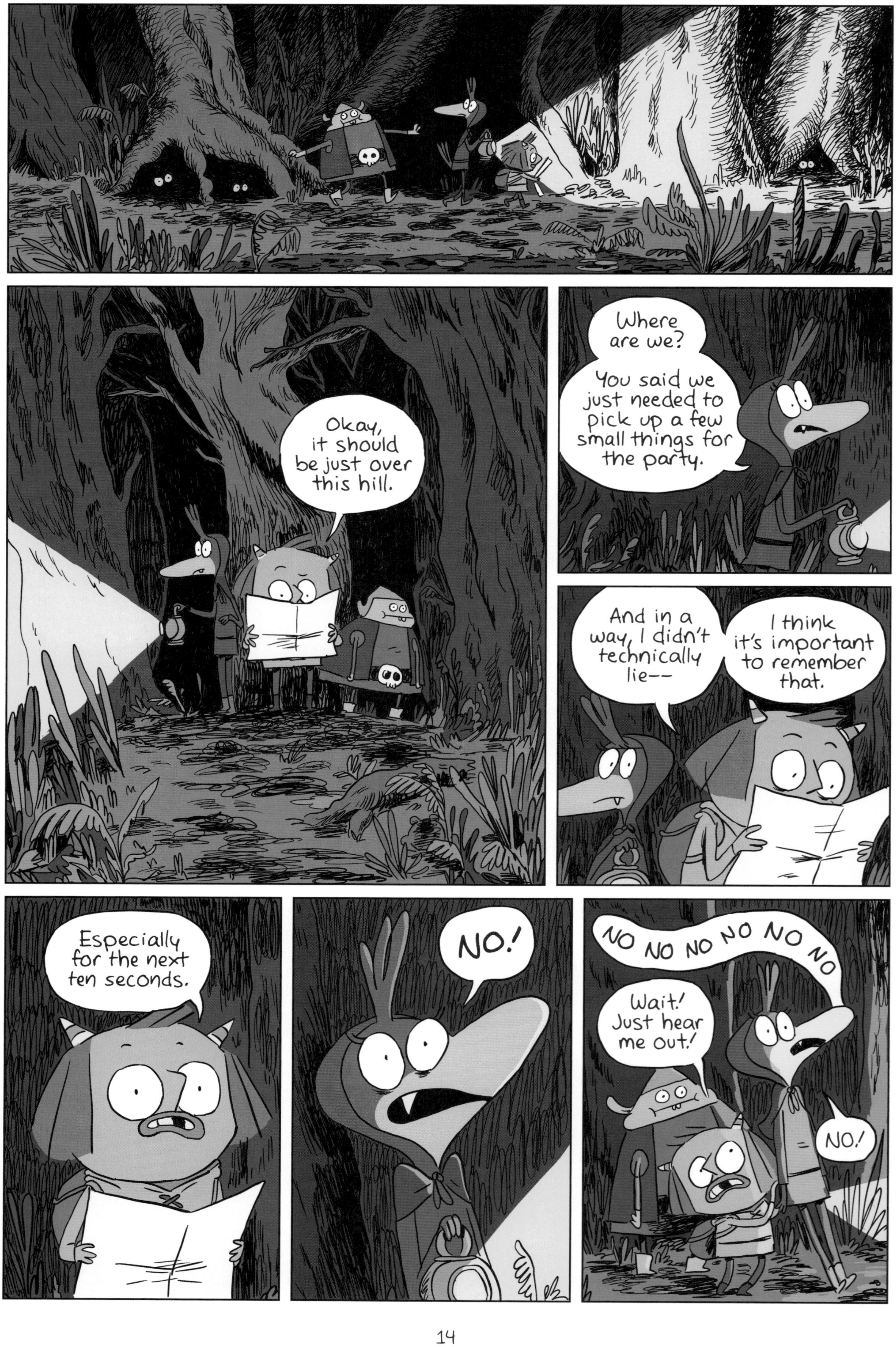
Okay, it should be just over this hill.
Where are we?
You said we just needed to pick up a few small things for the party.
And in a way, I didn't technically lie--
I think it's important to remember that.
Especially for the next ten seconds.
NO!
NO NO NO NO NO NO
Wait! Just hear me out!
NO!

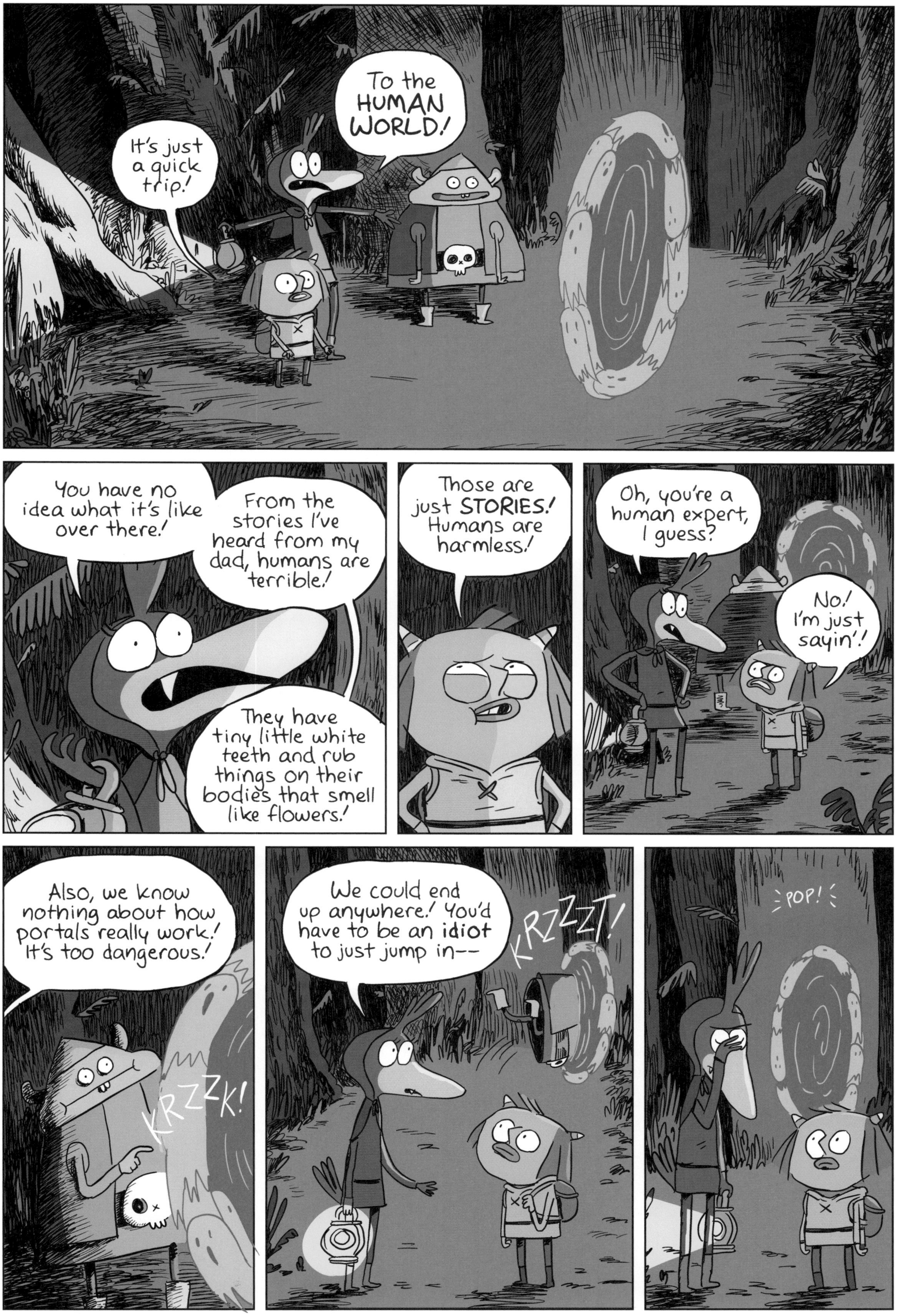

It's just a quick trip!
To the HUMAN WORLD!
You have no idea what it's like over there!
From the stories I've heard from my dad, humans are terrible!
They have tiny little white teeth and rub things on their bodies that smell like flowers!
Those are just STORIES! Humans are harmless!
Oh, you're a human expert, I guess?
No! I'm just sayin'!
Also, we know nothing about how portals really work! It's too dangerous!
KRZZZK!
We could end up anywhere! You'd have to be an idiot to just jump in--
KRZZZT!
POP!

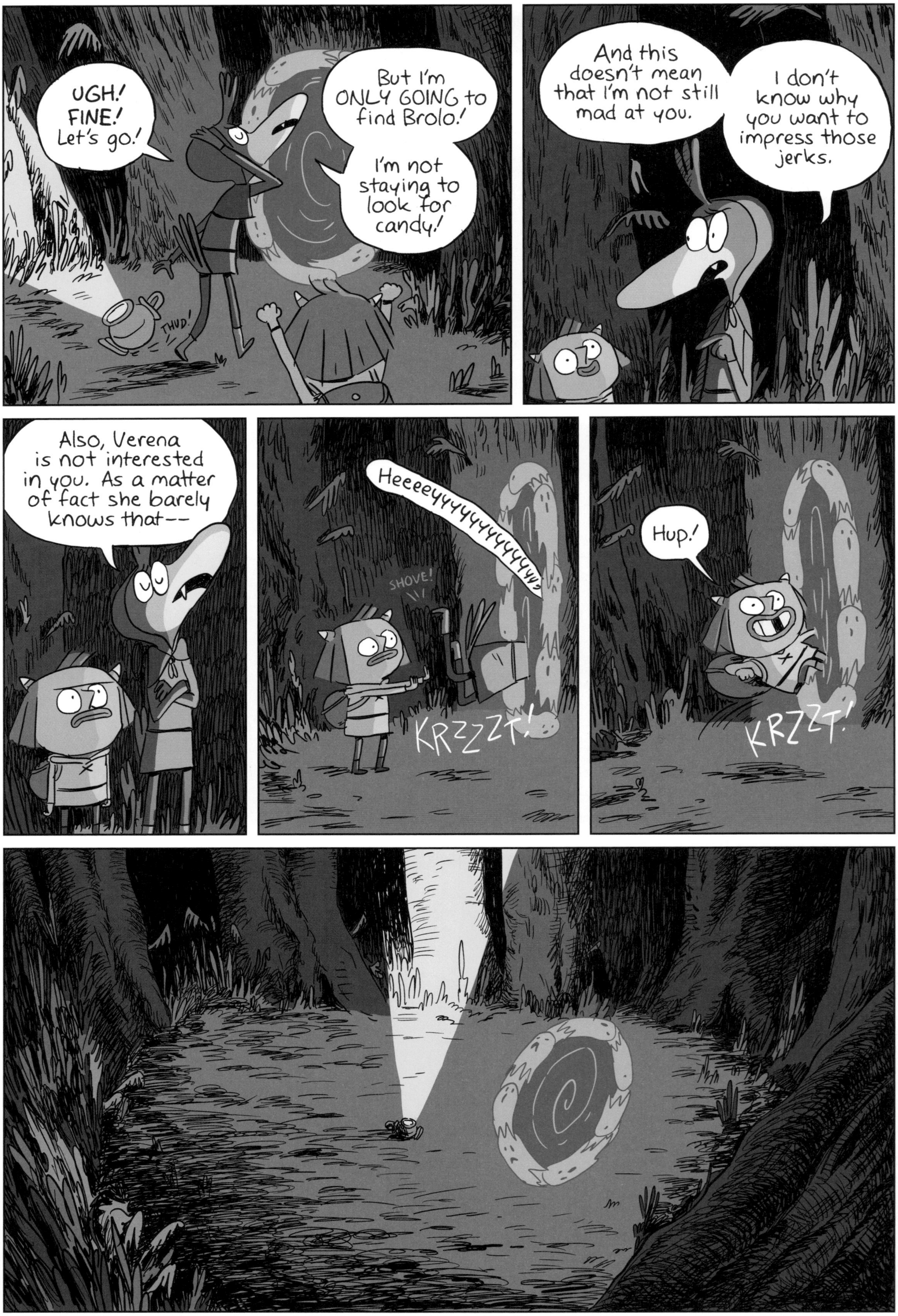
UGH! FINE! Let's go!
THUD!
But I'm ONLY GOING to find Brolo!
I'm not staying to look for candy!
And this doesn't mean that I'm not still mad at you.
I don't know why you want to impress those jerks.
Also, Verena is not interested in you. As a matter of fact she barely knows that--
SHOVE!
Heeeeyyyyyyyyyyyyyy
KRZZZT!
Hup!
KRZZZT!

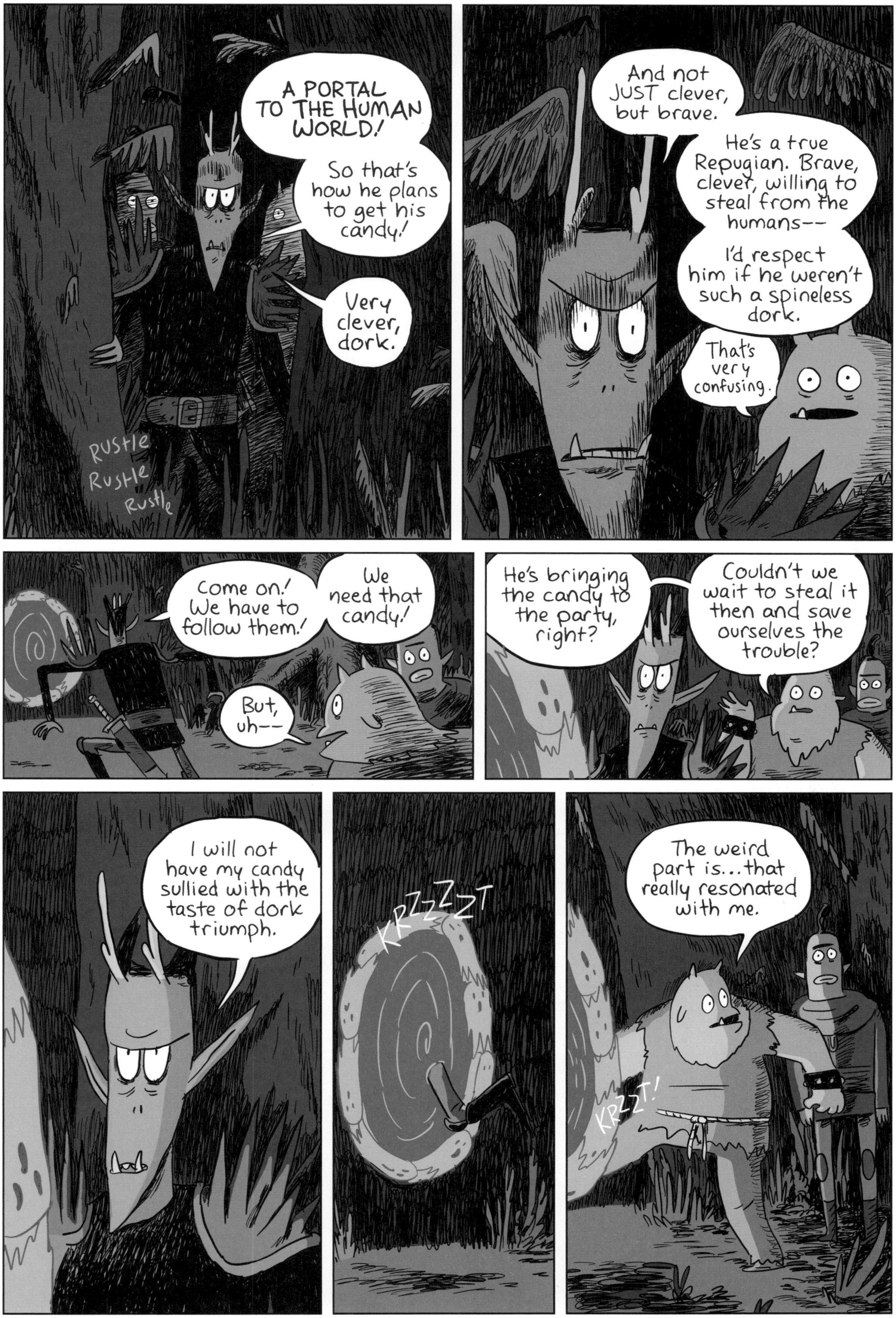
A PORTAL TO THE HUMAN WORLD!
So that's how he plans to get his candy!
Very clever, dork.
RUSTLE RUSTLE Rustle
And not JUST clever, but brave.
He's a true Repugian. Brave, clever, willing to steal from the humans--
I'd respect him if he weren't such a spineless dork.
That's very confusing.
Come on! We have to follow them!
We need that candy!
But, uh--
He's bringing the candy to the party, right?
Couldn't we wait to steal it then and save ourselves the trouble?
I will not have my candy sullied with the taste of dork triumph.
KRZZZZT
The weird part is... that really resonated with me.
KRZZT!

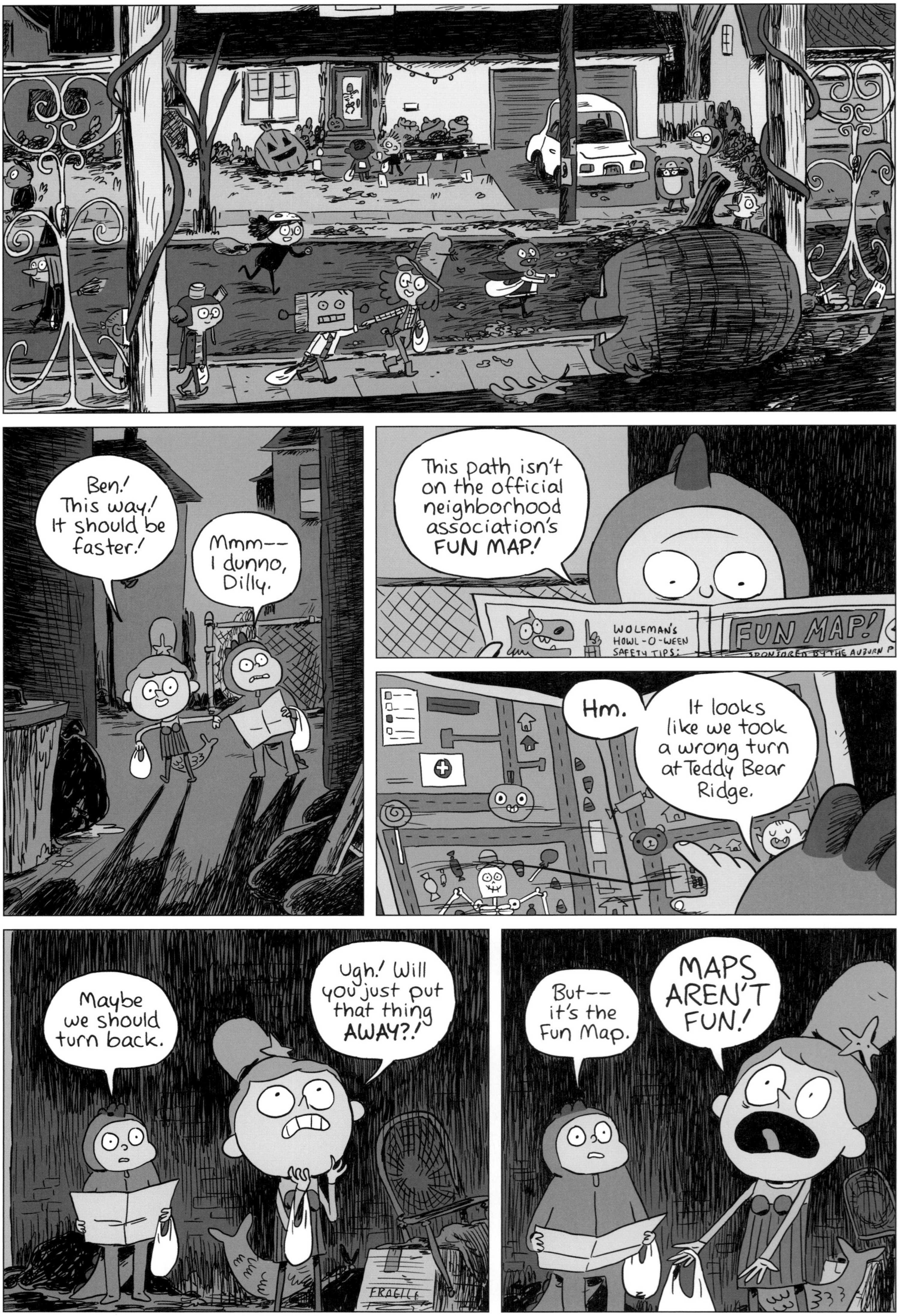
Ben! This way! It should be faster!
Mmm-- I dunno, Dilly.
This path isn't on the official neighborhood association's **FUN MAP!**
WOLFMAN'S HOWL-O-WEEN SAFETY TIPS:
FUN MAP!
Hm.
It looks like we took a wrong turn at Teddy Bear Ridge.
Maybe we should turn back.
Ugh! Will you just put that thing **AWAY?!**
FRAGILE
But-- it's the Fun Map.
MAPS AREN'T FUN!

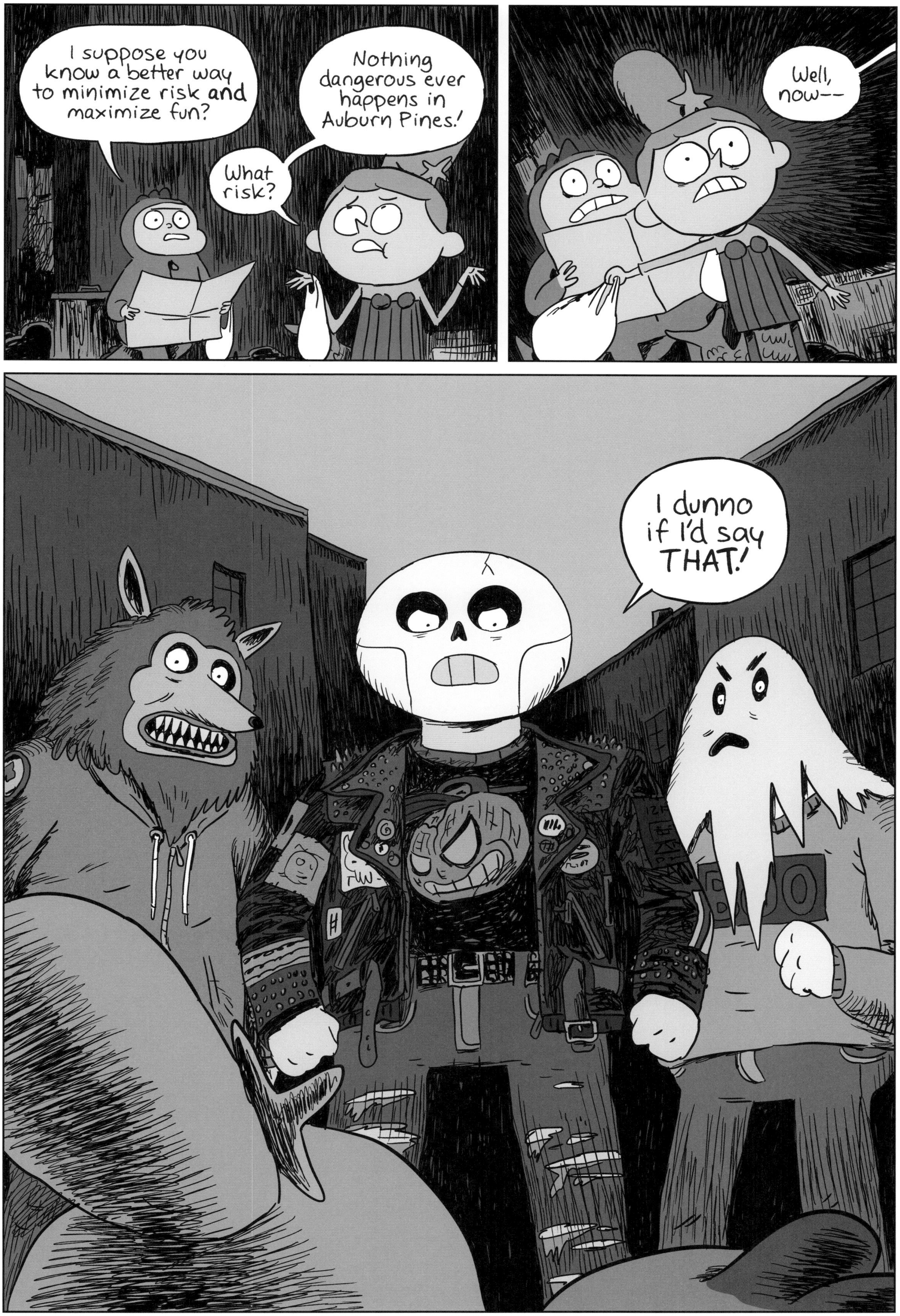
I suppose you know a better way to minimize risk and maximize fun?
What risk?
Nothing dangerous ever happens in Auburn Pines!
Well, now--
I dunno if I'd say THAT!

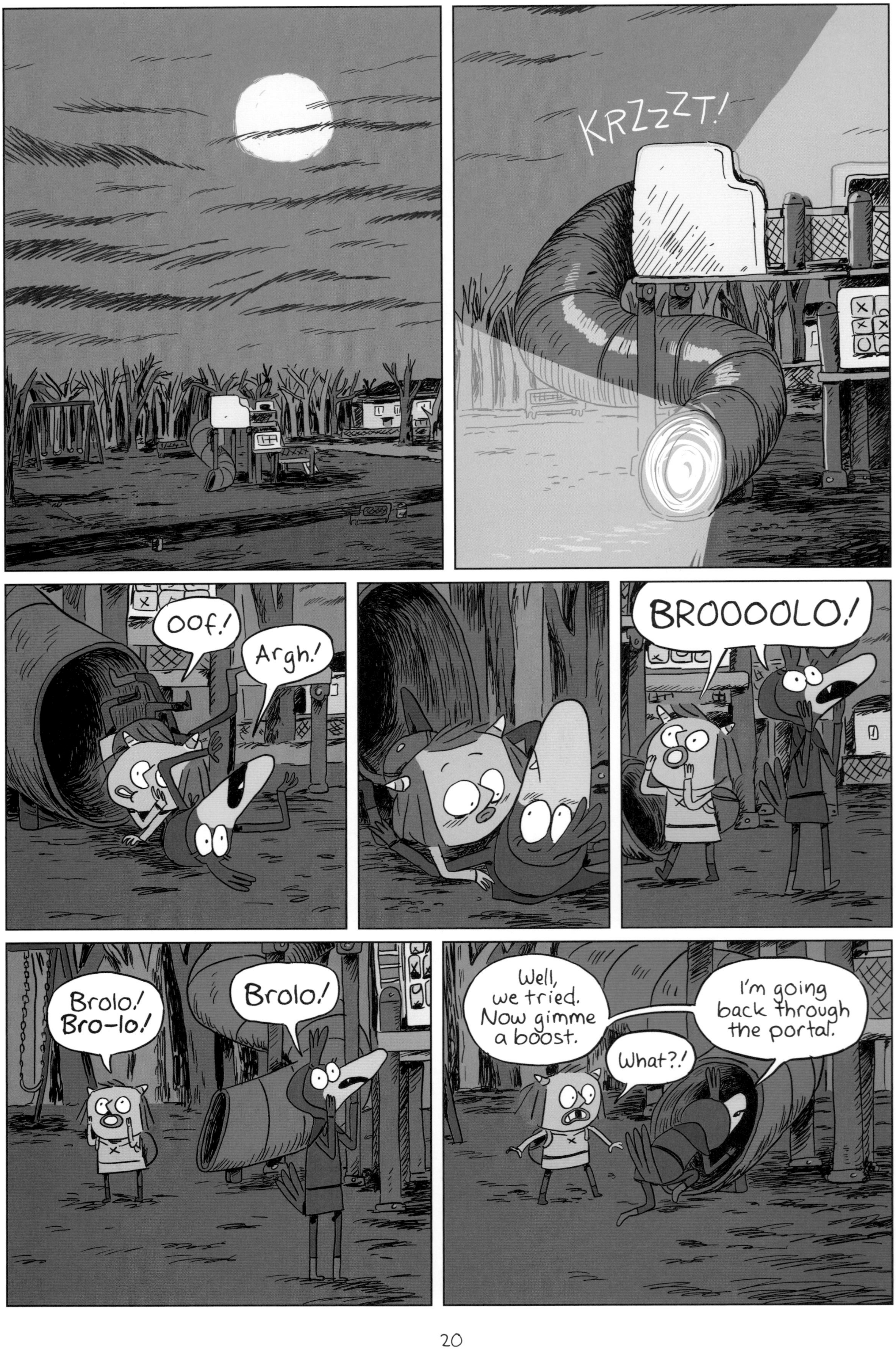
KRZzZT!
Oof!
Argh!
BROOOOLO!
Brolo! Bro-lo!
Brolo!
Well, we tried. Now gimme a boost.
What?!
I'm going back through the portal.

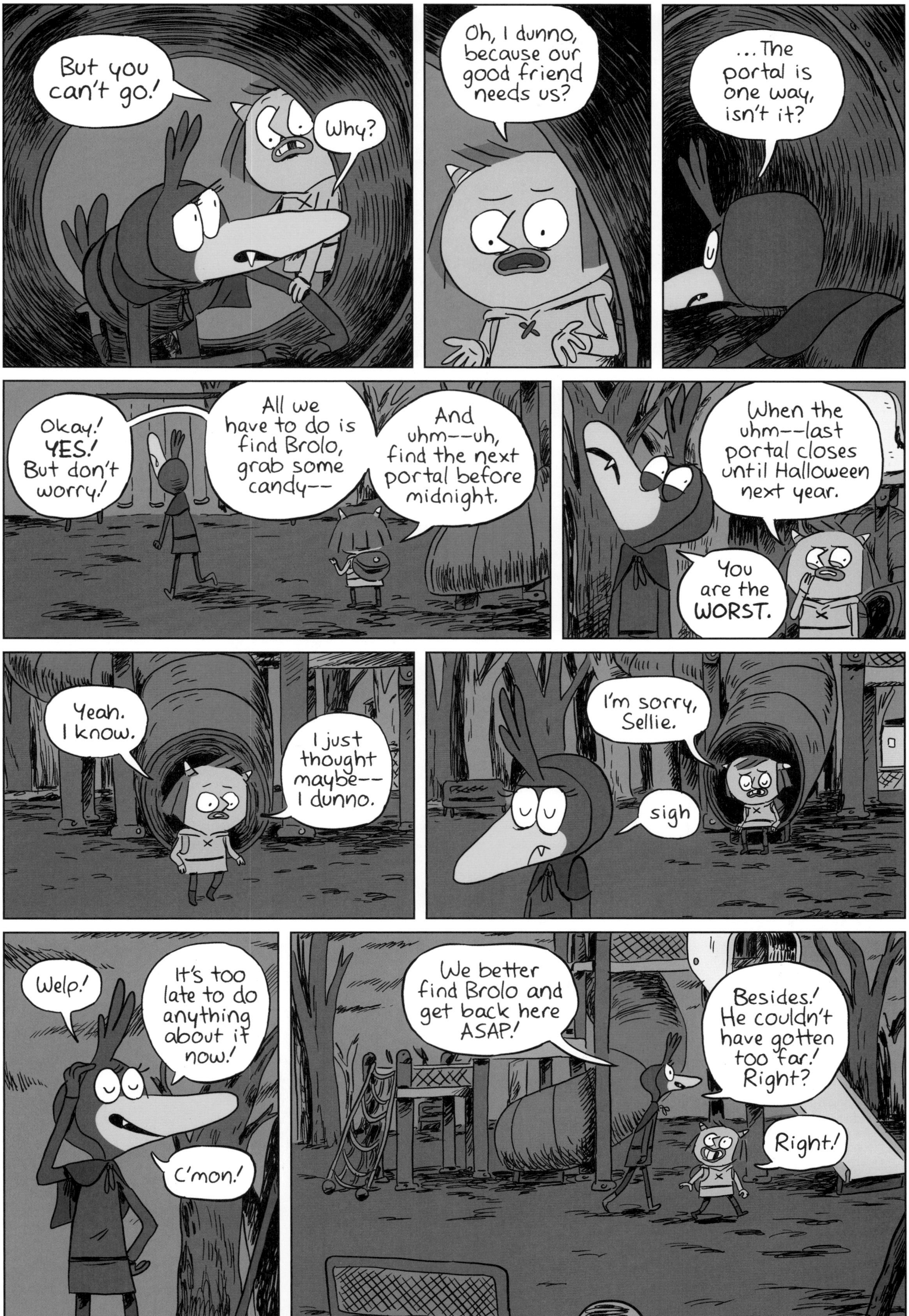
But you can't go!
Why?
Oh, I dunno, because our good friend needs us?
...The portal is one way, isn't it?
Okay! YES! But don't worry!
All we have to do is find Brolo, grab some candy--
And uhm--uh, find the next portal before midnight.
When the uhm--last portal closes until Halloween next year.
You are the WORST.
Yeah. I know.
I just thought maybe-- I dunno.
I'm sorry, Sellie.
sigh
Welp!
It's too late to do anything about it now!
C'mon!
We better find Brolo and get back here ASAP!
Besides! He couldn't have gotten too far! Right?
Right!

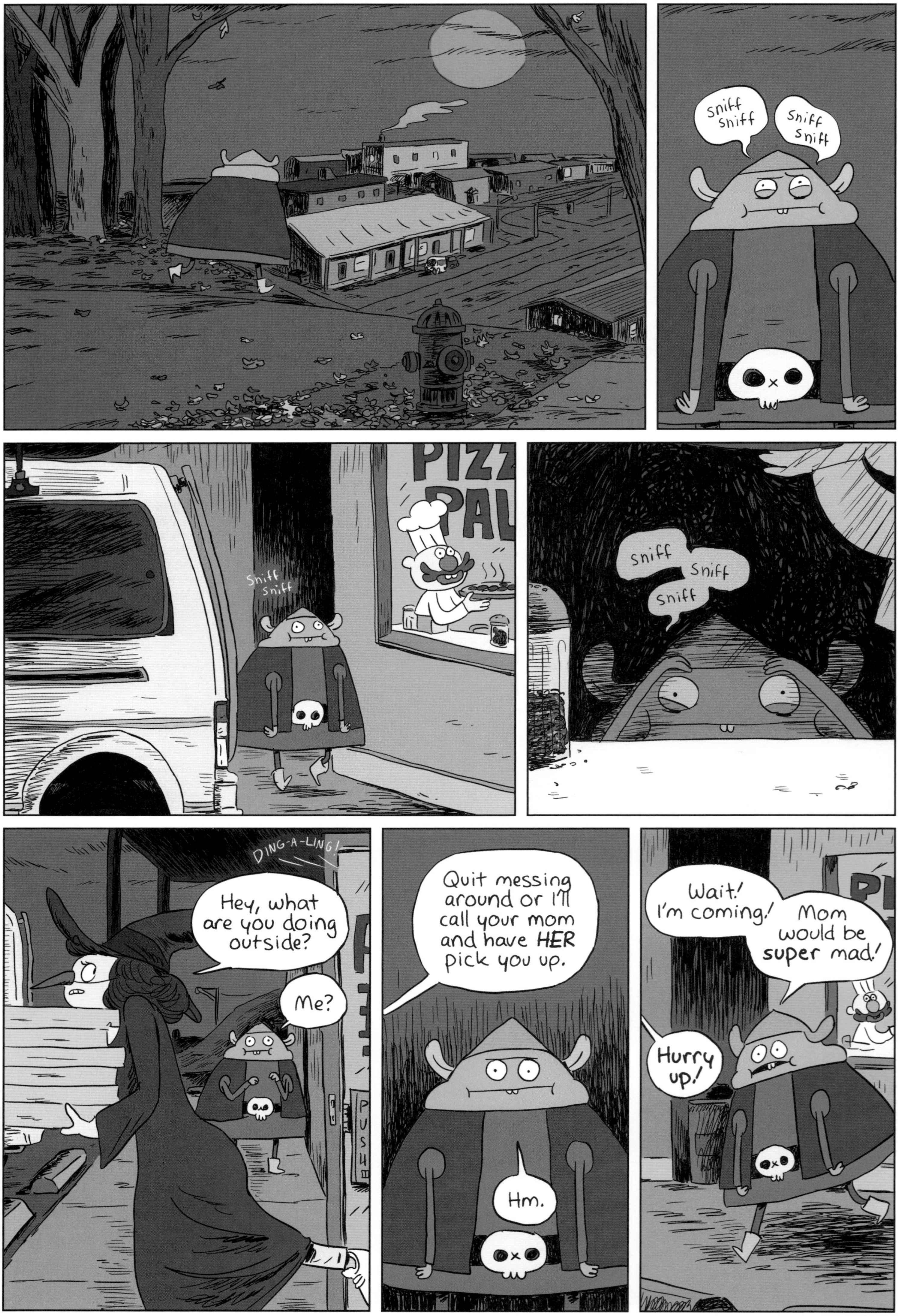
sniff sniff
Sniff sniff
PIZZ PAL
Sniff sniff
sniff
Sniff
sniff
DING-A-LING!
Hey, what are you doing outside?
Me?
PUSH
Quit messing around or I'll call your mom and have **HER** pick you up.
Hm.
Wait! I'm coming!
Mom would be **super** mad!
Hurry up!

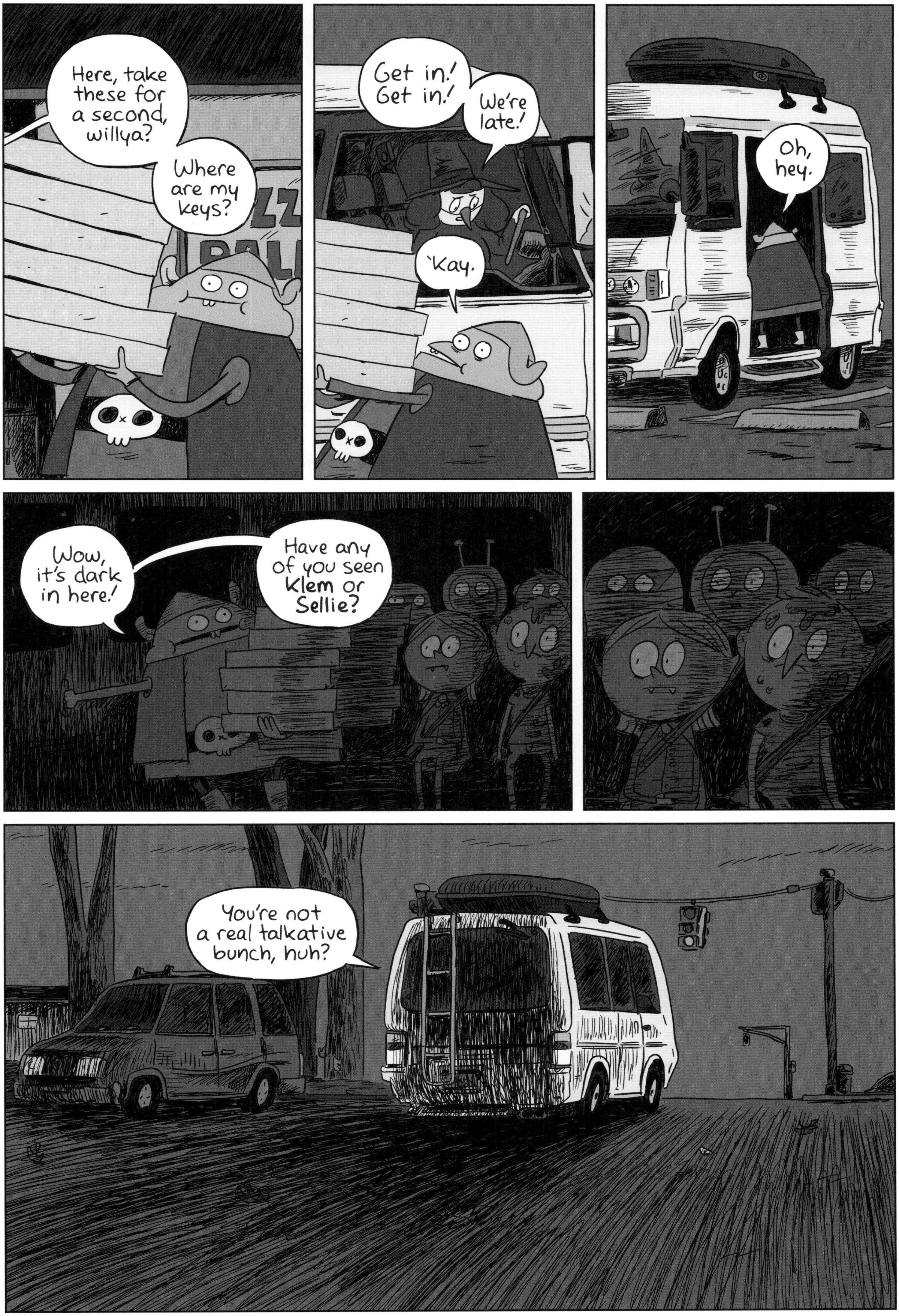
Here, take these for a second, willya?
Where are my keys?
Get in! Get in!
We're late!
'Kay.
Oh, hey.
Wow, it's dark in here!
Have any of you seen **Klem** or **Sellie**?
You're not a real talkative bunch, huh?

24

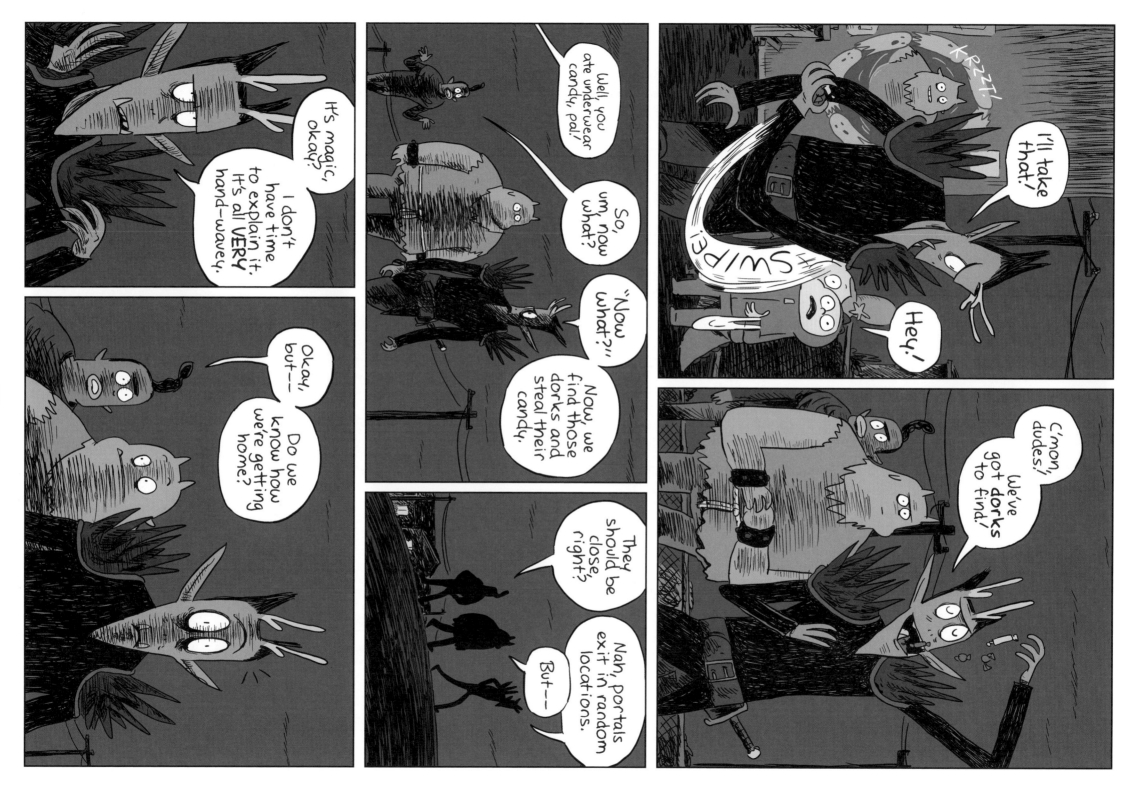

27

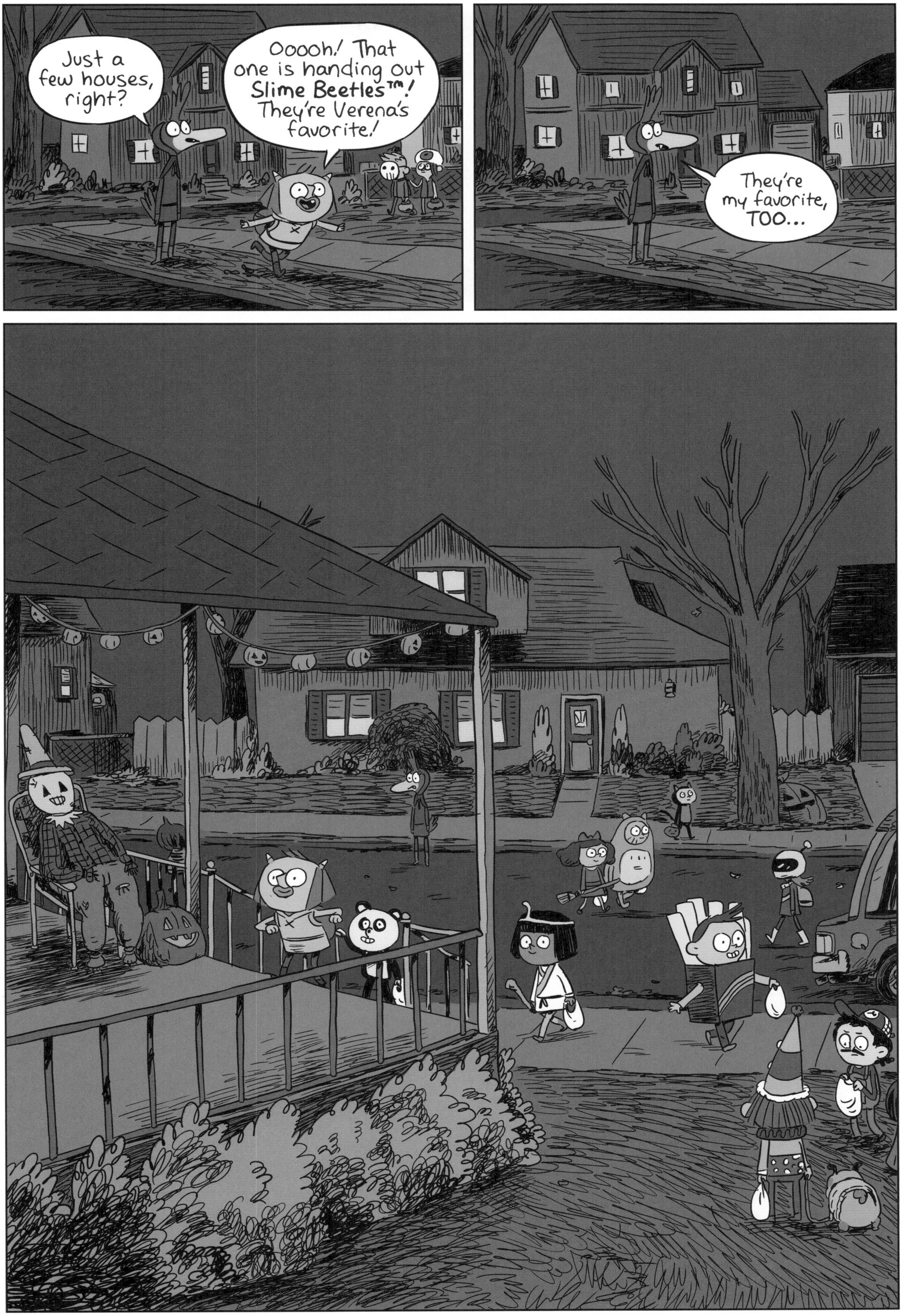
Just a few houses, right?
Ooooh! That one is handing out Slime Beetles™! They're Verena's favorite!
They're my favorite, TOO...

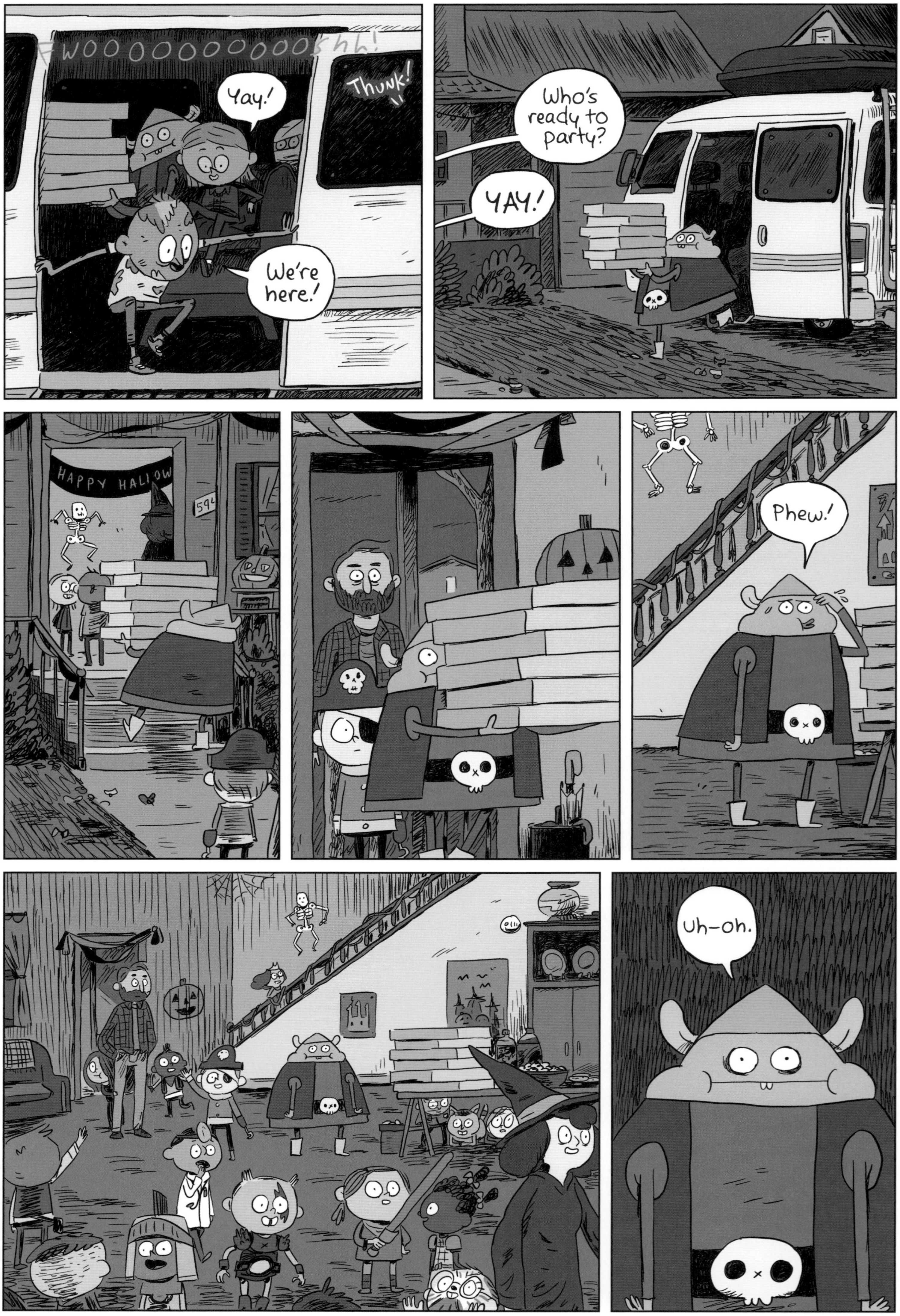
FWOOOOOOOOOOOshh!
Yay!
Thunk!
We're here!
Who's ready to party?
YAY!
HAPPY HALLOW
Phew!
Uh-oh.

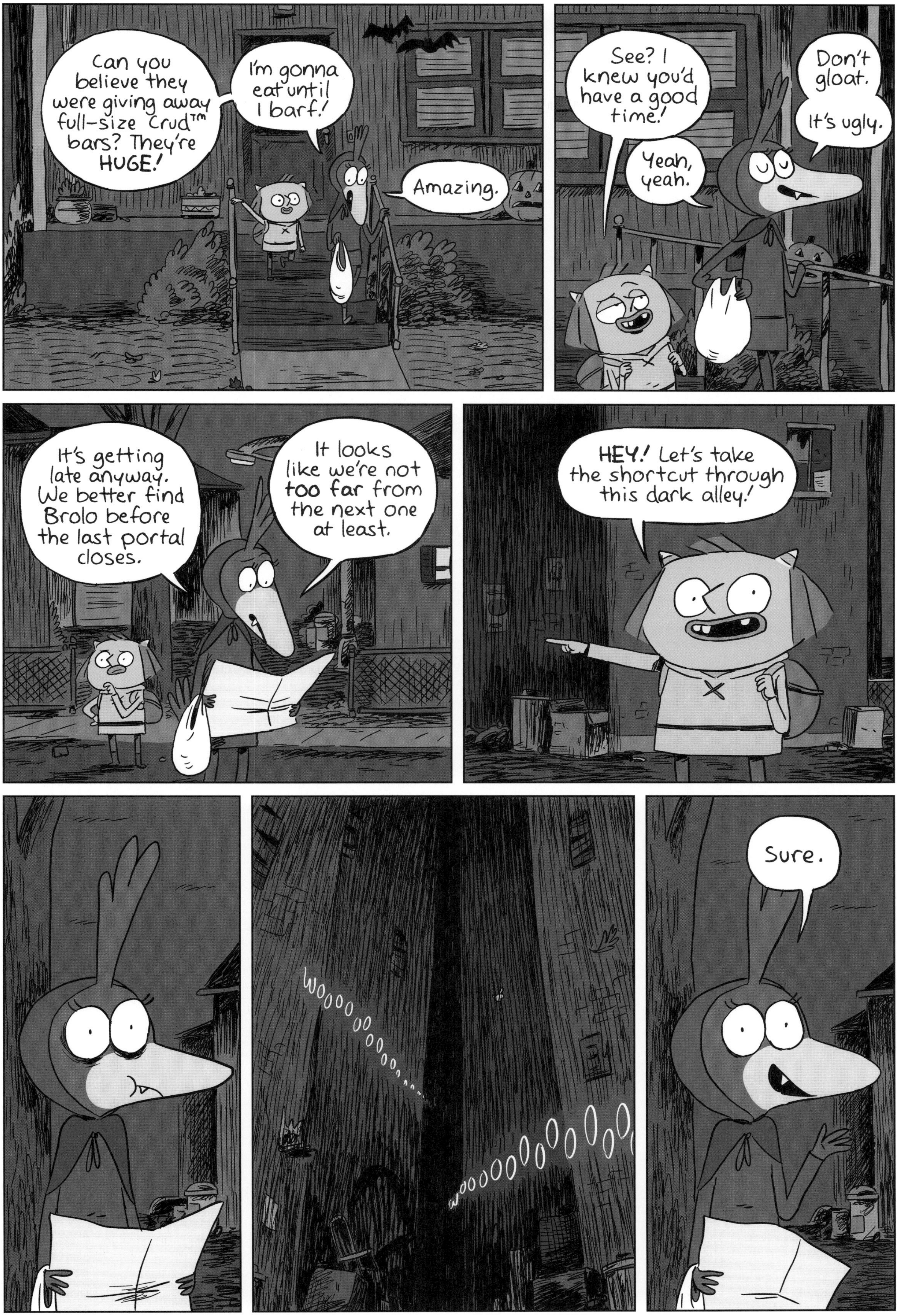
Can you believe they were giving away full-size Crud™ bars? They're **HUGE!**
I'm gonna eat until I barf!
Amazing.
See? I knew you'd have a good time!
Yeah, yeah.
Don't gloat.
It's ugly.
It's getting late anyway. We better find Brolo before the last portal closes.
It looks like we're not **too far** from the next one at least.
HEY! Let's take the shortcut through this dark alley!
Wooooooooooo...
wooooooooooOOOO
Sure.

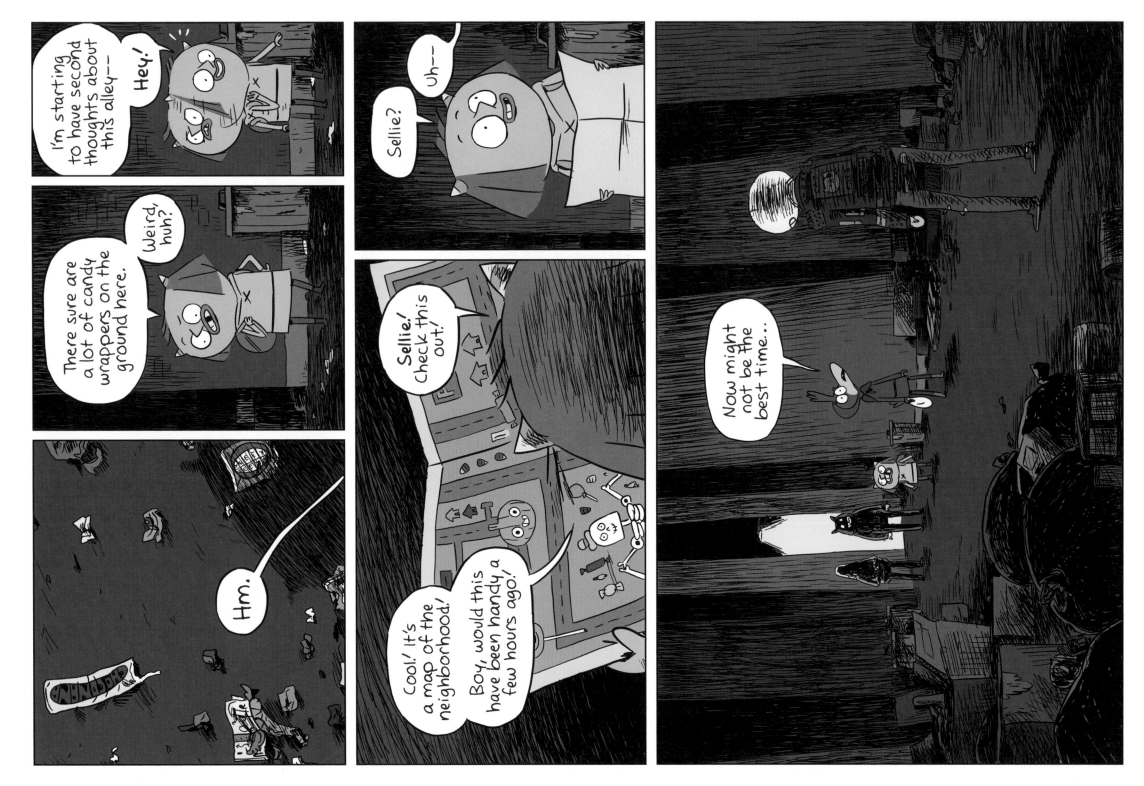

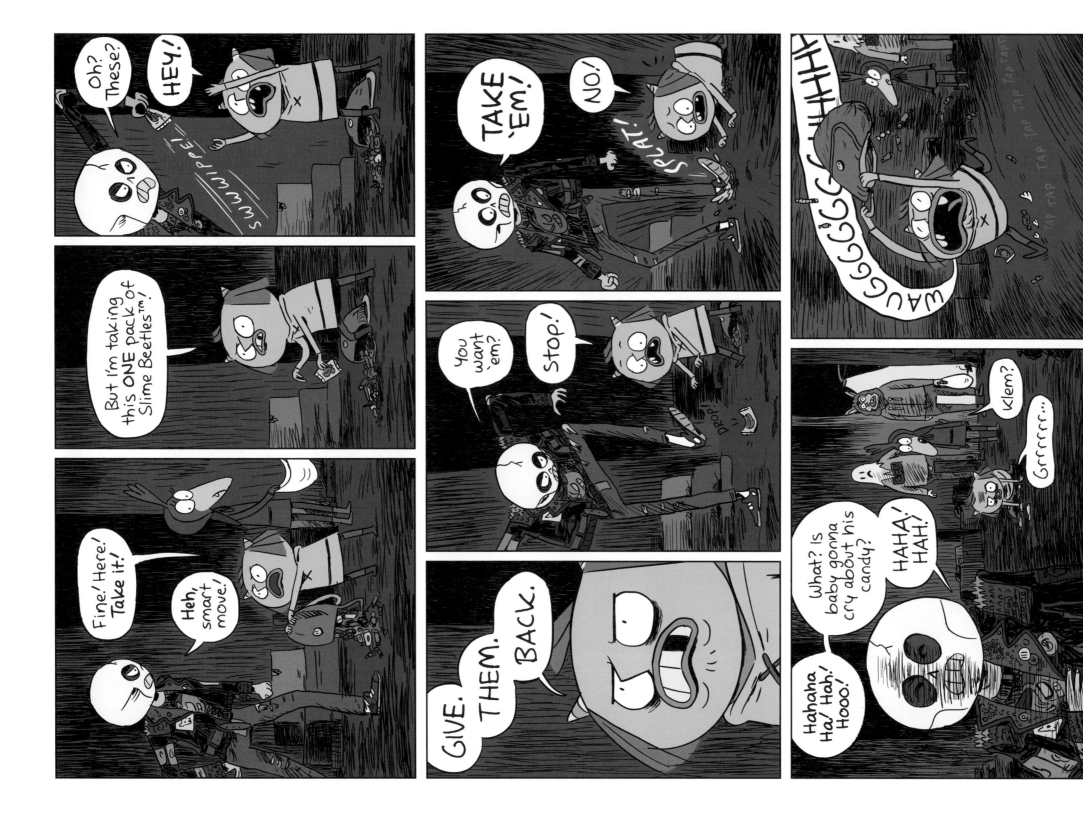

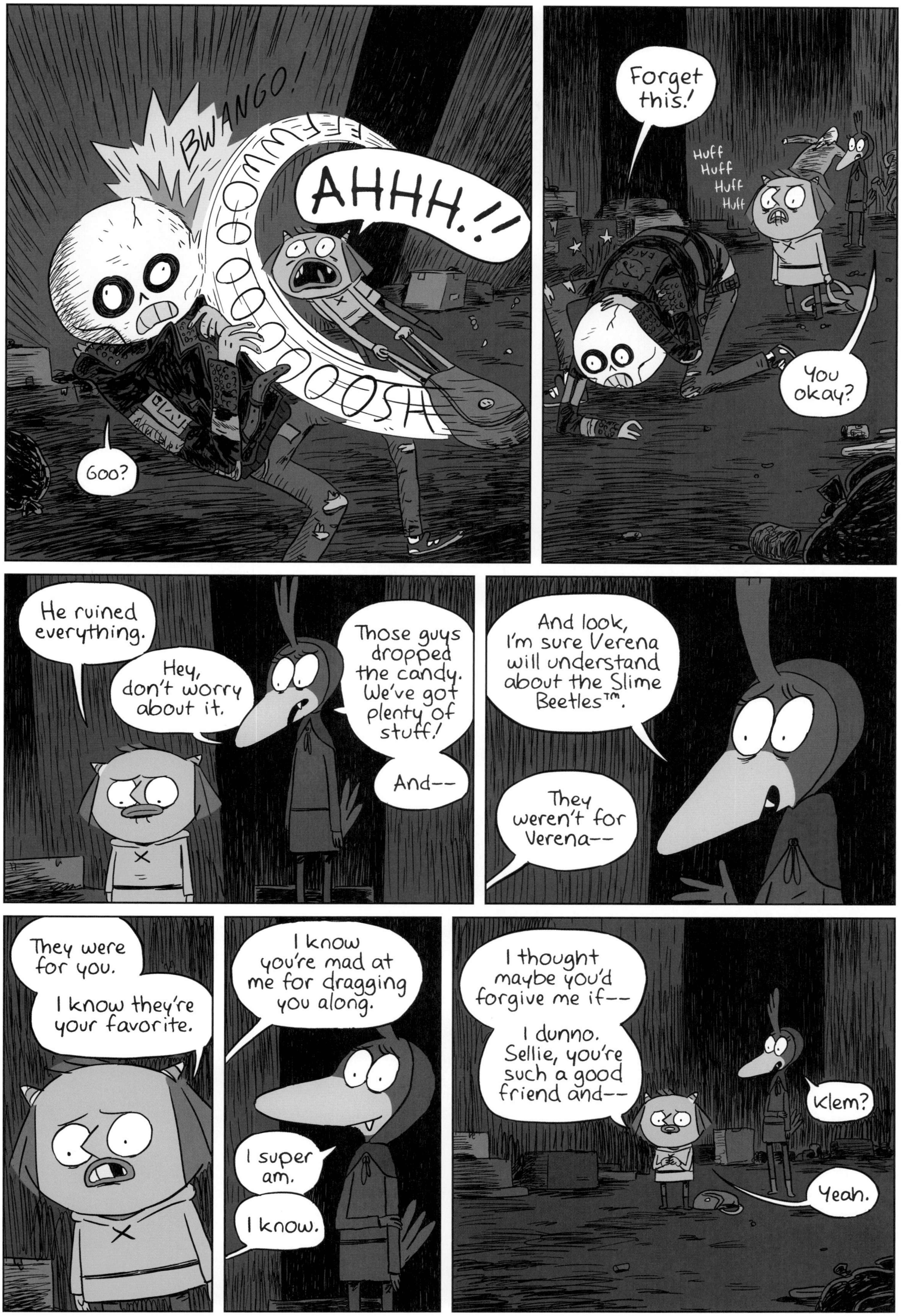
BWANGO!
FFWOOOOOOOOOSH
AHHH.!!
Goo?
Forget this!
Huff Huff Huff Huff
You okay?
He ruined everything.
Hey, don't worry about it.
Those guys dropped the candy. We've got plenty of stuff!
And--
And look, I'm sure Verena will understand about the Slime Beetles™.
They weren't for Verena--
They were for you.
I know they're your favorite.
I know you're mad at me for dragging you along.
I super am.
I know.
I thought maybe you'd forgive me if--
I dunno. Sellie, you're such a good friend and--
Klem?
Yeah.

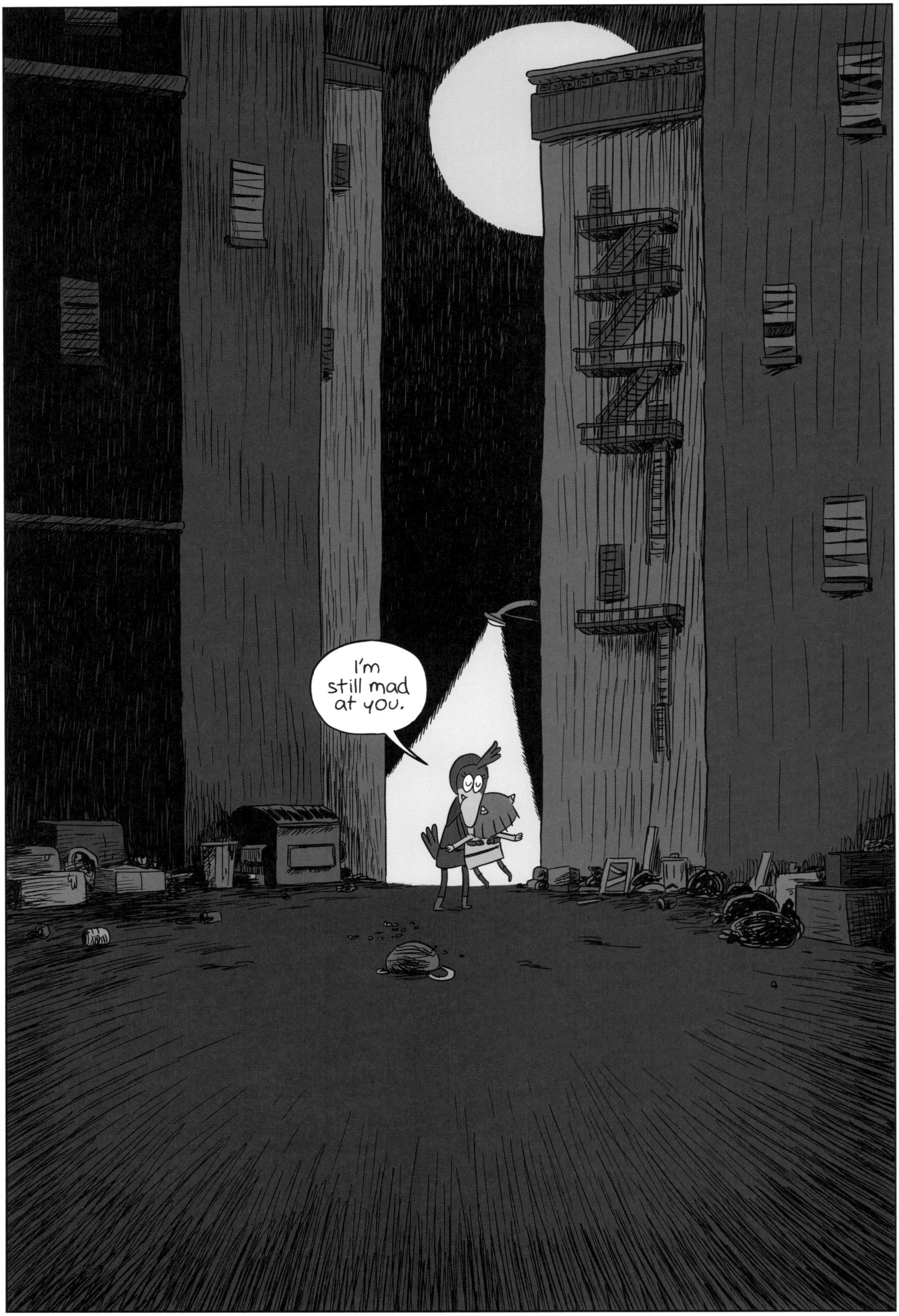
I'm still mad at you.

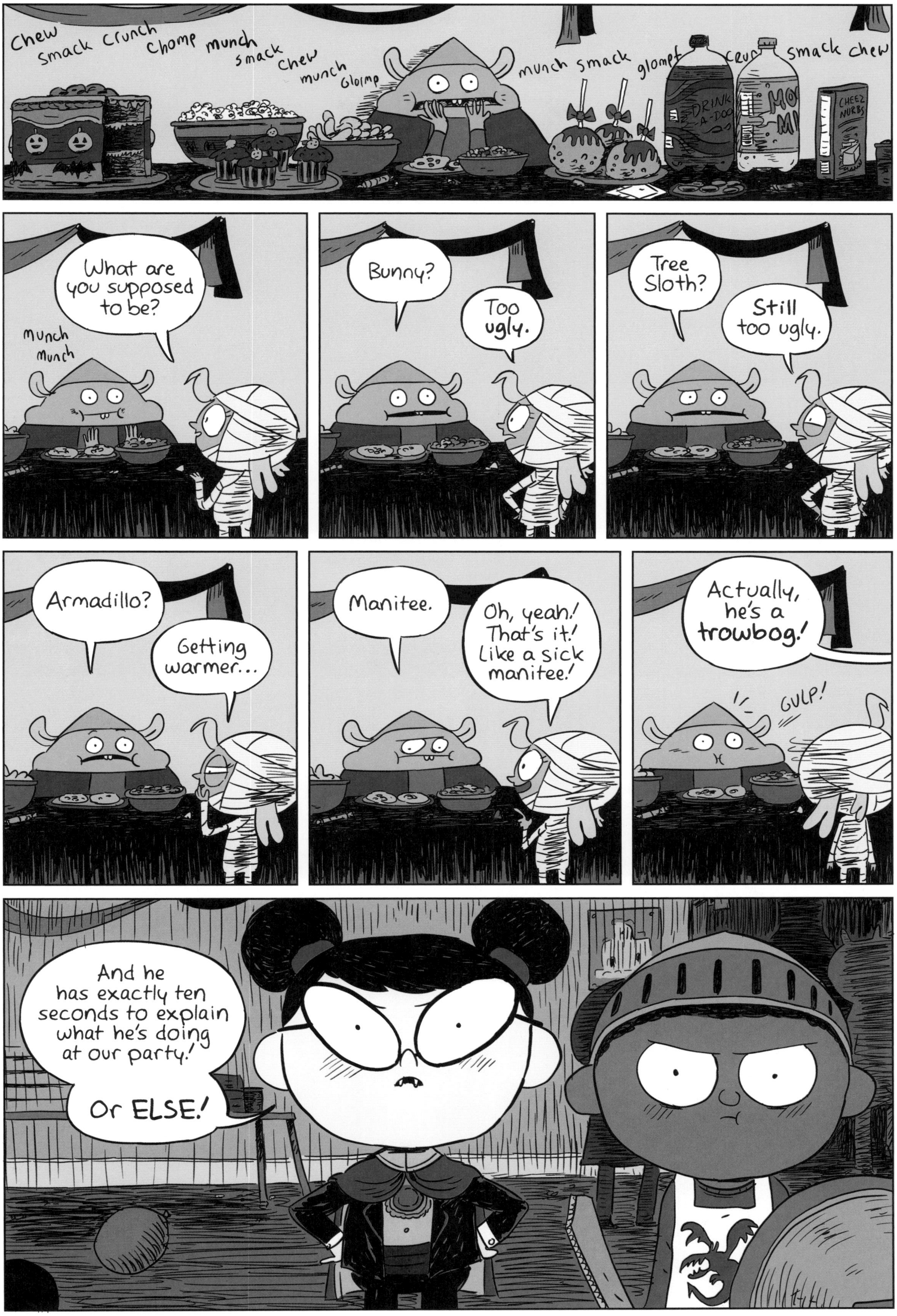
Chew smack crunch chomp munch smack chew munch Glomp
munch smack glompf crun smack chew
DRINK-A-DOO
CHEEZ NURBS
What are you supposed to be?
munch munch
Bunny?
Too ugly.
Tree Sloth?
Still too ugly.
Armadillo?
Getting warmer...
Manitee.
Oh, yeah! That's it! Like a sick manitee!
Actually, he's a trowbog!
GULP!
And he has exactly ten seconds to explain what he's doing at our party!
Or ELSE!

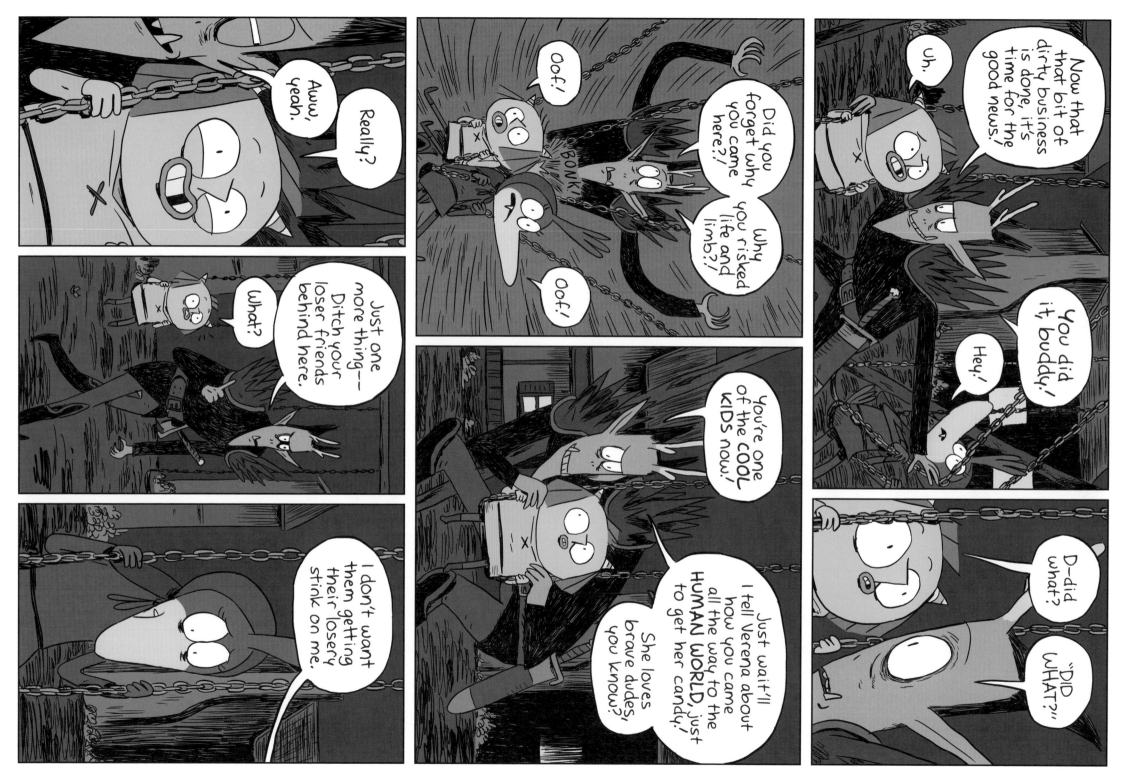

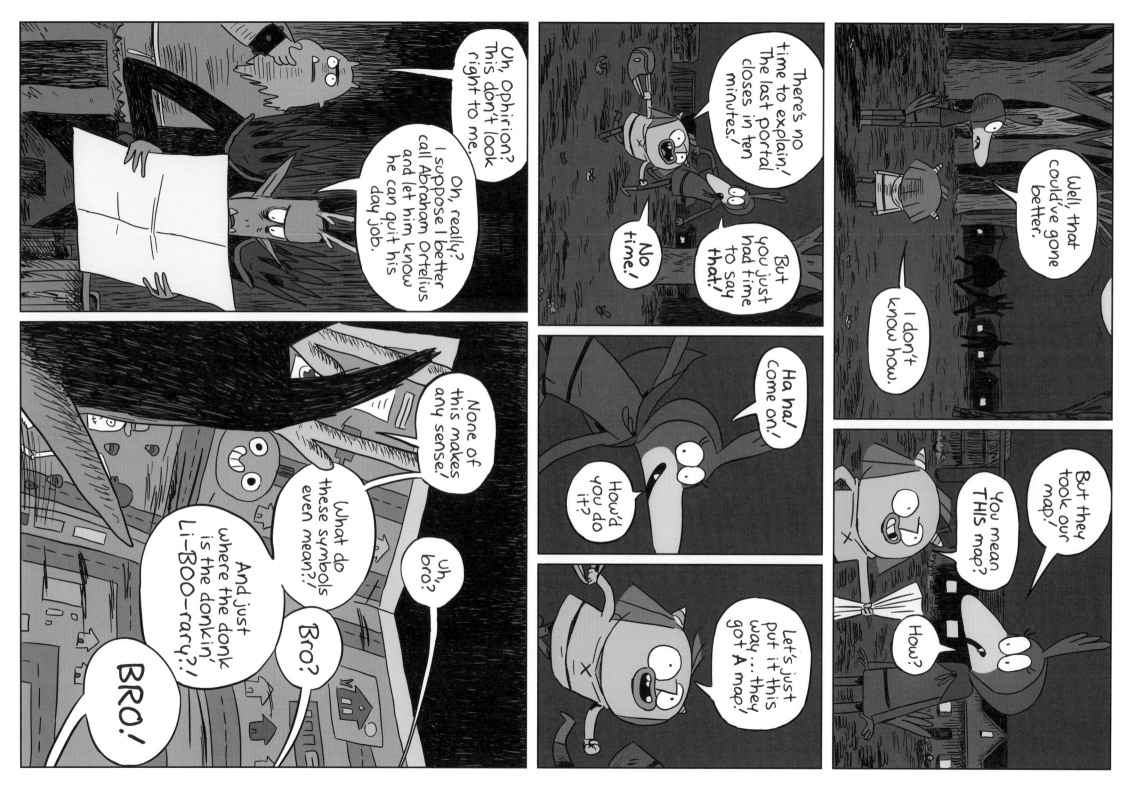

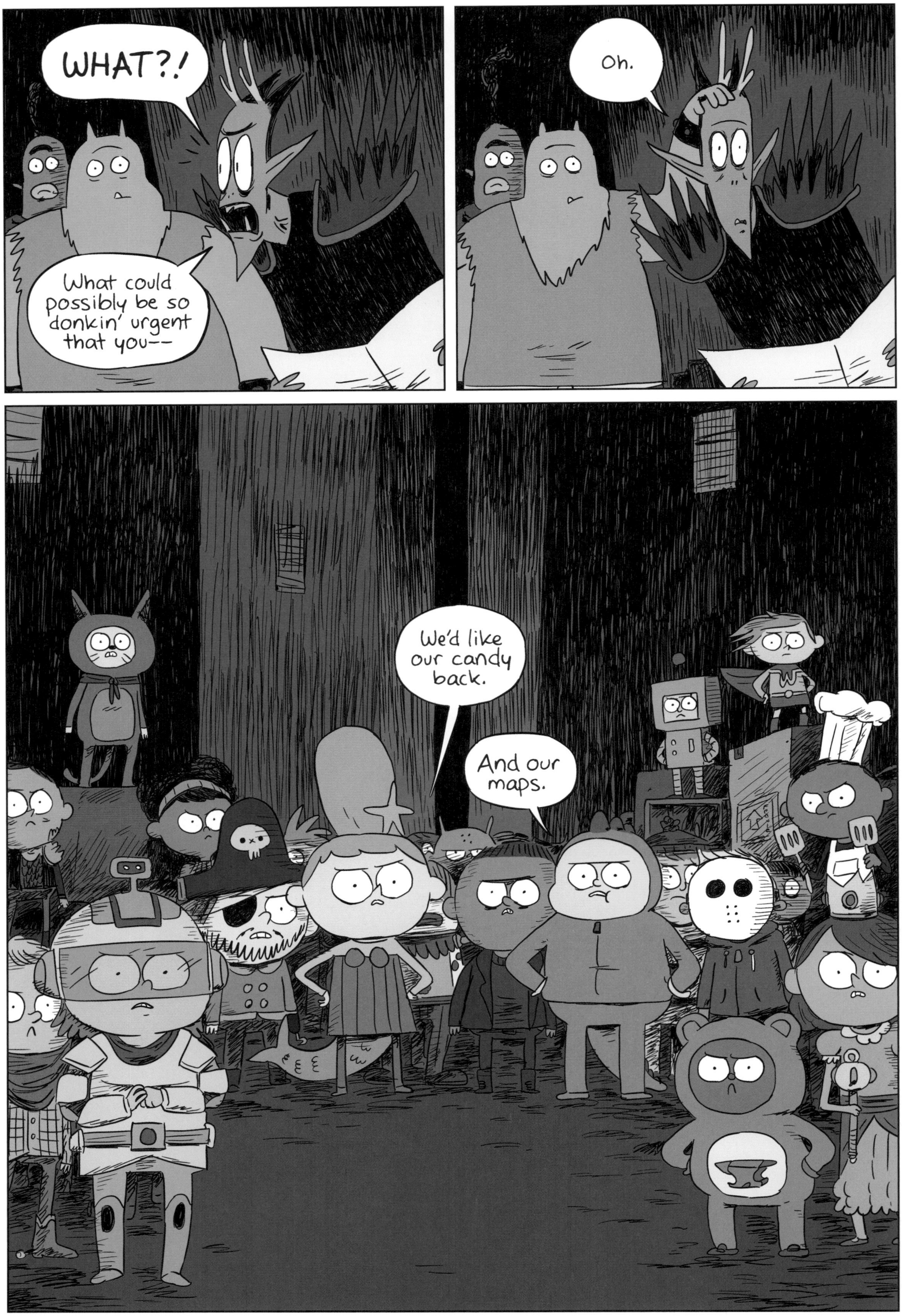
WHAT?!
What could possibly be so donkin' urgent that you--
Oh.
We'd like our candy back.
And our maps.

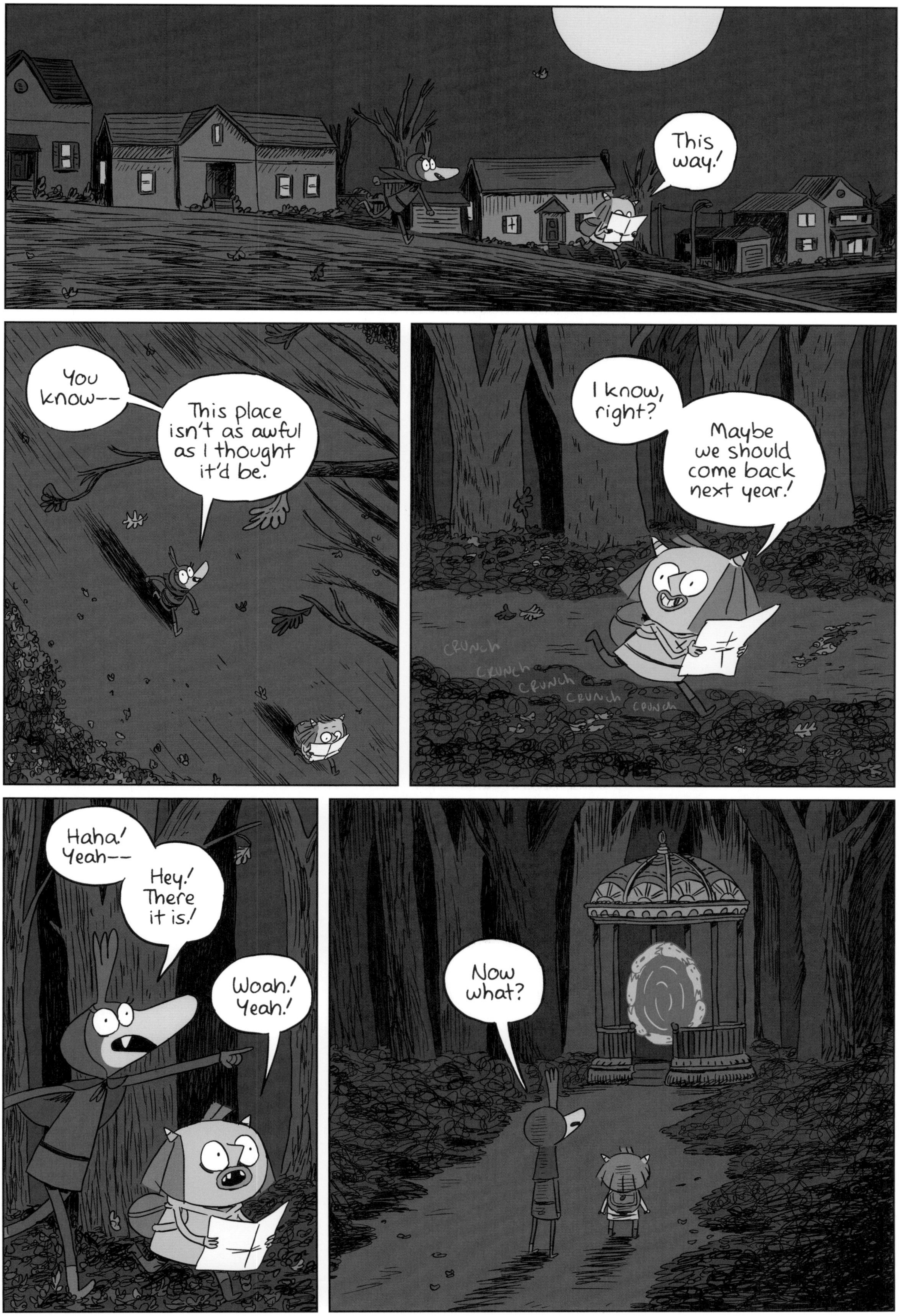
This way!
You know--
This place isn't as awful as I thought it'd be.
I know, right?
Maybe we should come back next year!
CRUNCH CRUNCH CRUNCH CRUNCH CRUNCH
Haha! Yeah--
Hey! There it is!
Woah! Yeah!
Now what?

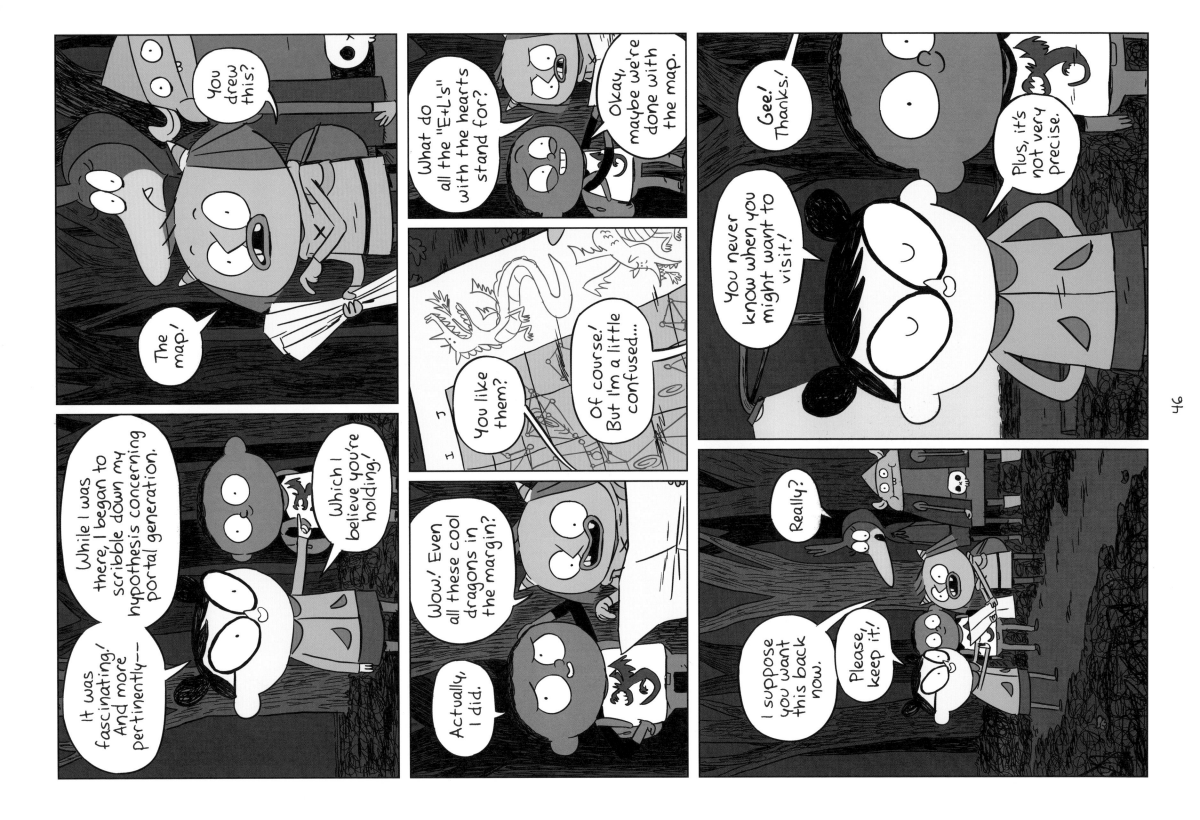

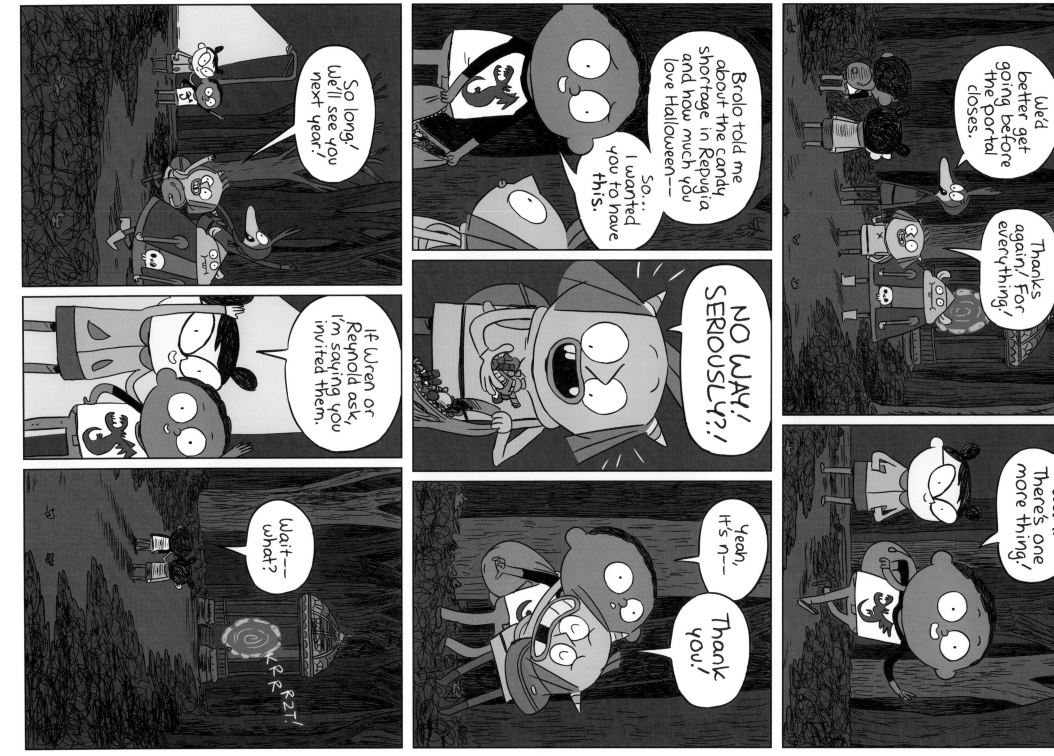

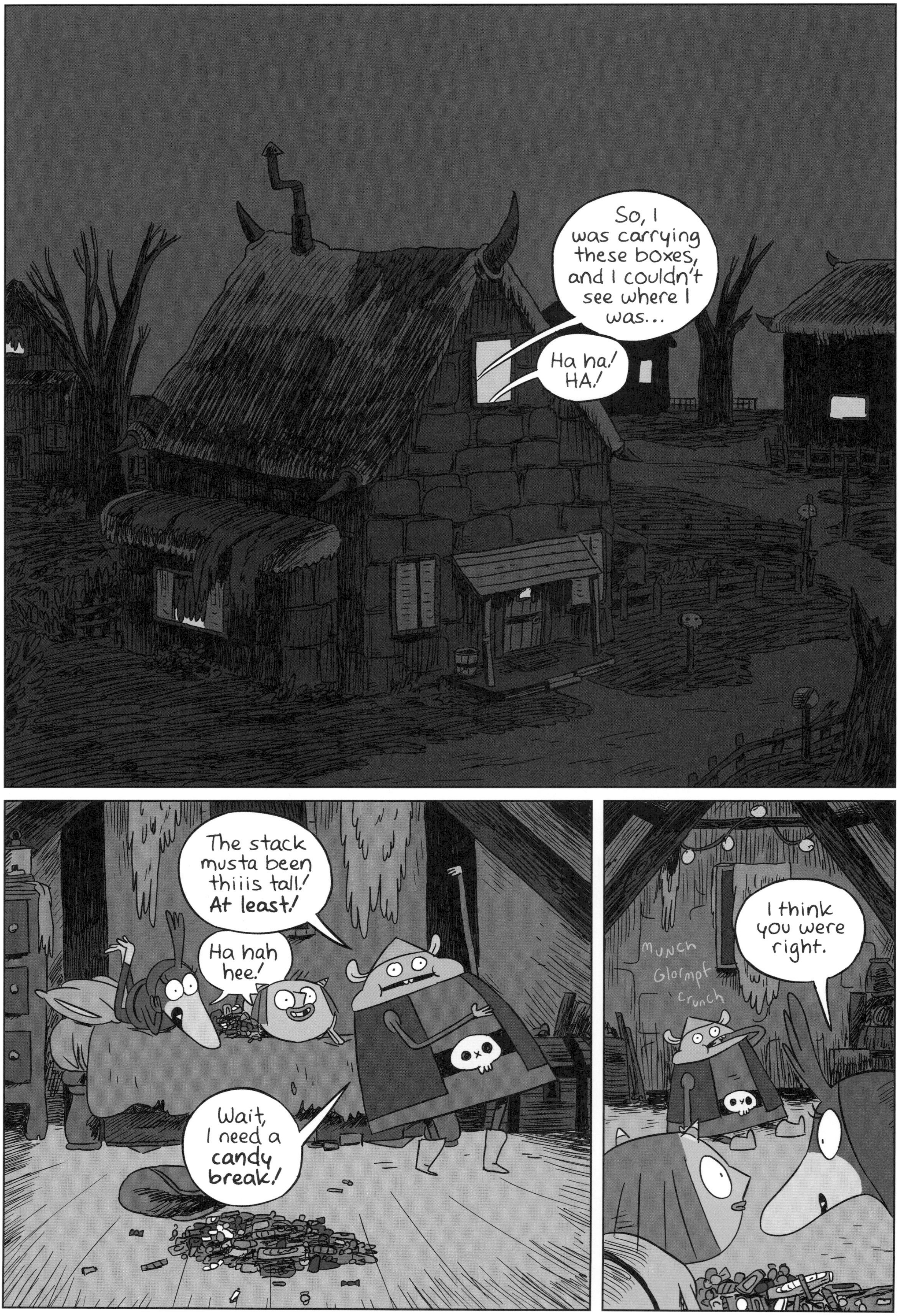
So, I was carrying these boxes, and I couldn't see where I was...
Ha ha! HA!
The stack musta been thiiis tall! At least!
Ha hah hee!
Wait, I need a candy break!
Munch
Glormpf
crunch
I think you were right.

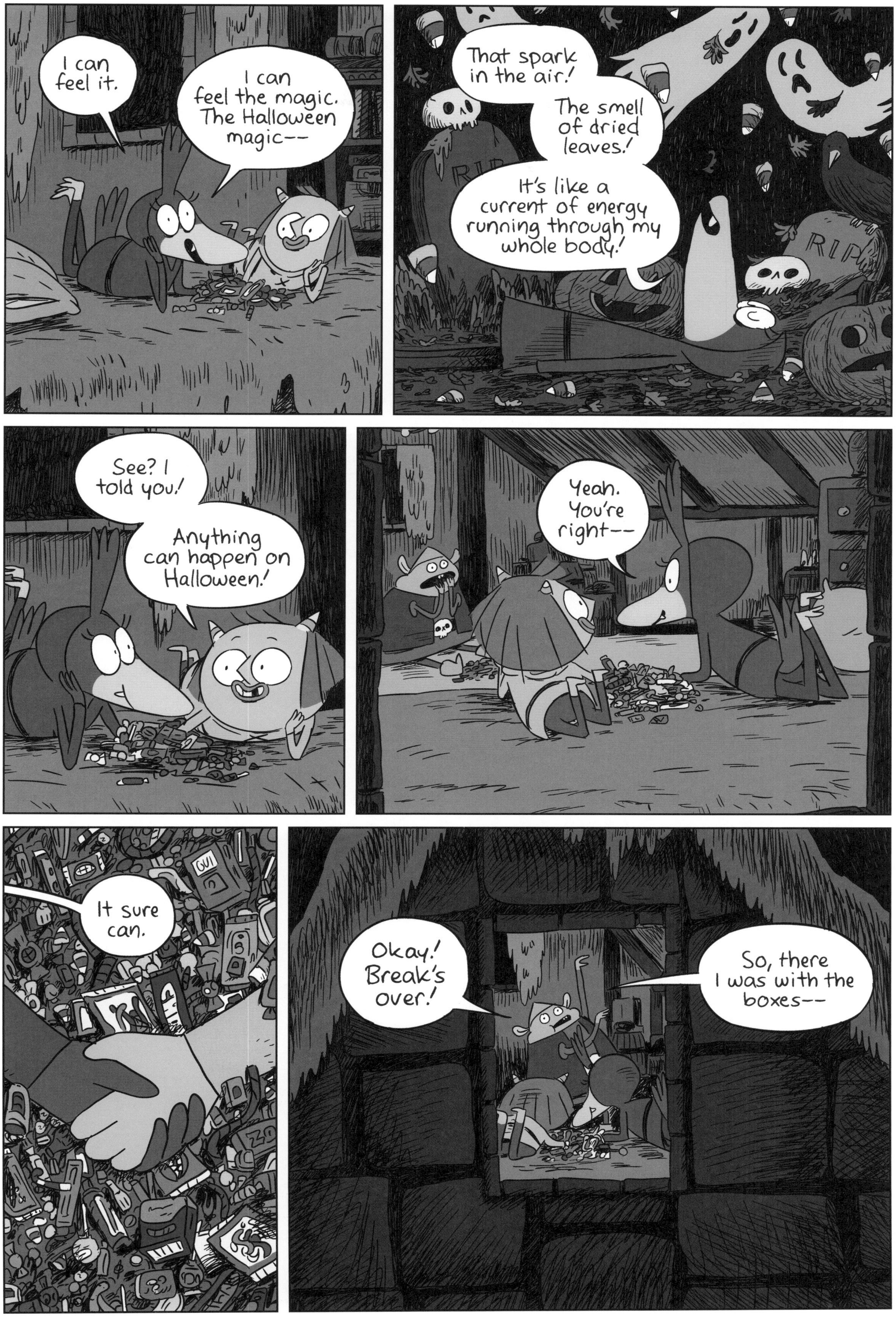
I can feel it.
I can feel the magic. The Halloween magic--
That spark in the air!
The smell of dried leaves!
It's like a current of energy running through my whole body!
See? I told you!
Anything can happen on Halloween!
Yeah. You're right--
It sure can.
Okay! Break's over!
So, there I was with the boxes--
RIP
RIP

AFTERWORD

By TASHA SOUNART

HALLOWEEN has always been my favorite holiday. Not because of the scary parts (I was always more on the trembly side) but because of the creativity behind it. Halloween is the one day of the year when everyone can run around as whatever they want to be, whether it's something scary, cute, powerful, or funny. People allow themselves to try on new personas that could be completely different from how they are in everyday life.

As a child, I always thought the setting of Halloween would make a very cool game. There were just so many things I loved about it — the exploration of the darkened neighborhood with a pack of friends, the brightly lit pumpkins on all the doorsteps, the slight smell of smoke coming from the chimneys, the crunch of fallen leaves underfoot. Oh, and there was always the intense candy trading session that followed. For the entire year afterward, I would carefully ration out my candy so it would last me until the next Halloween. Of course I would have to hide it from my sister, who would go through her candy in a couple of days. Sometime around the age of 11, after I had received my beloved NES, I remember drawing a group of little pixelated characters trick-or-treating. Years later, at Double Fine, I got the opportunity to actually see my idea come to life, which was simultaneously stressful and awesome.

During the project, a few things were very important to me: I wanted to keep the tone of the game funny, warm, family-friendly, and sincere — much like the Peanuts specials I loved while growing up. I wanted parents to be able to play the game along with their children, since this was the type of game I would have loved to play as a kid.

I also wanted the game to emphasize the contrast between the kids' more mundane, "normal" suburban lives, and the epic, powerful world of their imaginations. My mom would hand-make the costumes for my sister and I, so I wanted to include that crafting aspect in the game — the transformation of ordinary objects into costume pieces. Later in life, I would continue to construct my own elaborate outfits each year, even though I never learned how to sew (the glue gun is my friend). One of my proudest moments was in my 20s, when I won a contest at work with my homemade "garden gnome sitting on a hill" costume.

Another central idea in the game was that every character (boys and girls) had the ability to wear any of the costumes. As a tomboy growing up, I was often teased for liking "boy stuff." But on Halloween, I could be whatever I wanted, whether that was a space warrior, a magician, a unicorn, or a clown. Kids have fun exploring all sorts of identities and scenarios and shouldn't have limitations placed upon their imaginations.

After *Costume Quest* was released, a single page comic based on the game started making the rounds on Twitter and made its way to Double Fine. This is how I was introduced to the quirky and charming art of Zac Gorman. (I still want a print of that comic, by the way!) Zac's art style and sense of humor mesh perfectly with the game's universe, so I can't think of a better match for the graphic novel. In this book we get to explore more of how the Repugians experience the world — what would monster children think of Halloween and trick-or-treating?

Now that I have a son of my own, I'm so excited for him to experience everything I loved about Halloween growing up and can't wait to play the games with him. It's really awesome to see the *Costume Quest* universe continue to be explored, through both the game's sequel, and Zac's own interpretation of the world and the new characters he's created.

Tasha Sounart

Tasha Sounart (formerly Harris) is an animator and game designer who lives in San Francisco with her husband, son and two cats, Mr. Peterson and Snoopy. She was project lead on the game *Costume Quest*, which released in October 2010.

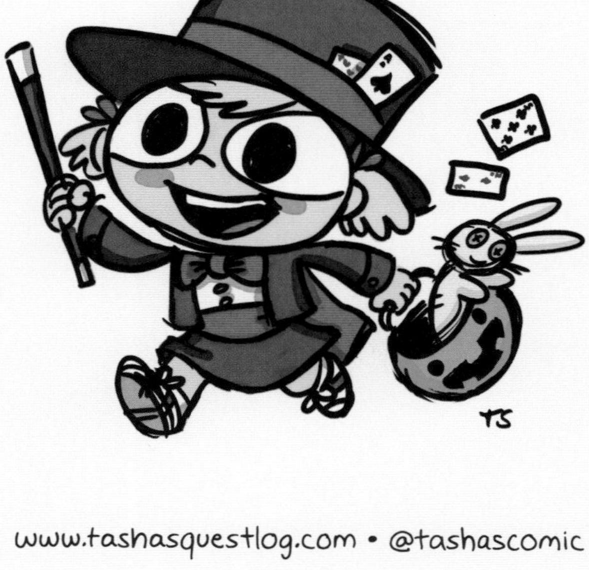
TS

www.tashasquestlog.com • @tashascomic

Zac Gorman is a cartoonist from Detroit, Michigan raised on the sacred suburban triumvirate of video games, cartoons, and comic books. He's the creator of the popular webcomic *Magical Game Time* and has worked on several animated television series as a storyboard artist and character designer. Zac currently resides in Chicago with his far more talented wife and a furry little monster who most people mistake for a cat.

magicalgametime.com • zacgorman.com • @zacgormania

Zac would like to thank Suzy for her love and affection, Gabe, Greg, Tim and everybody at Double Fine for their trust and encouragement, Charlie and the Oni team for all their hard work, Fangamer for their enthusiasm, and finally, Mom, Dad, Austin, Dave, Jason, and Erin for all their support along the way.

Trick-or-treat your way into these delicious video game goodies by Double Fine Productions!

COSTUME QUEST

PC, Mac, Linux, Xbox 360, PS3, iOS, Android

Rated E10+

COSTUME QUEST 2

PC, Mac, Linux, Xbox One, Xbox 360, Playstation 4, Playstation 3, Wii U

WWW.DOUBLEFINE.COM/GAMES

@doublefine

BROKEN AGE

PC, Mac, Linux, iOS, Android

WWW.BROKENAGEGAME.COM

@doublefine

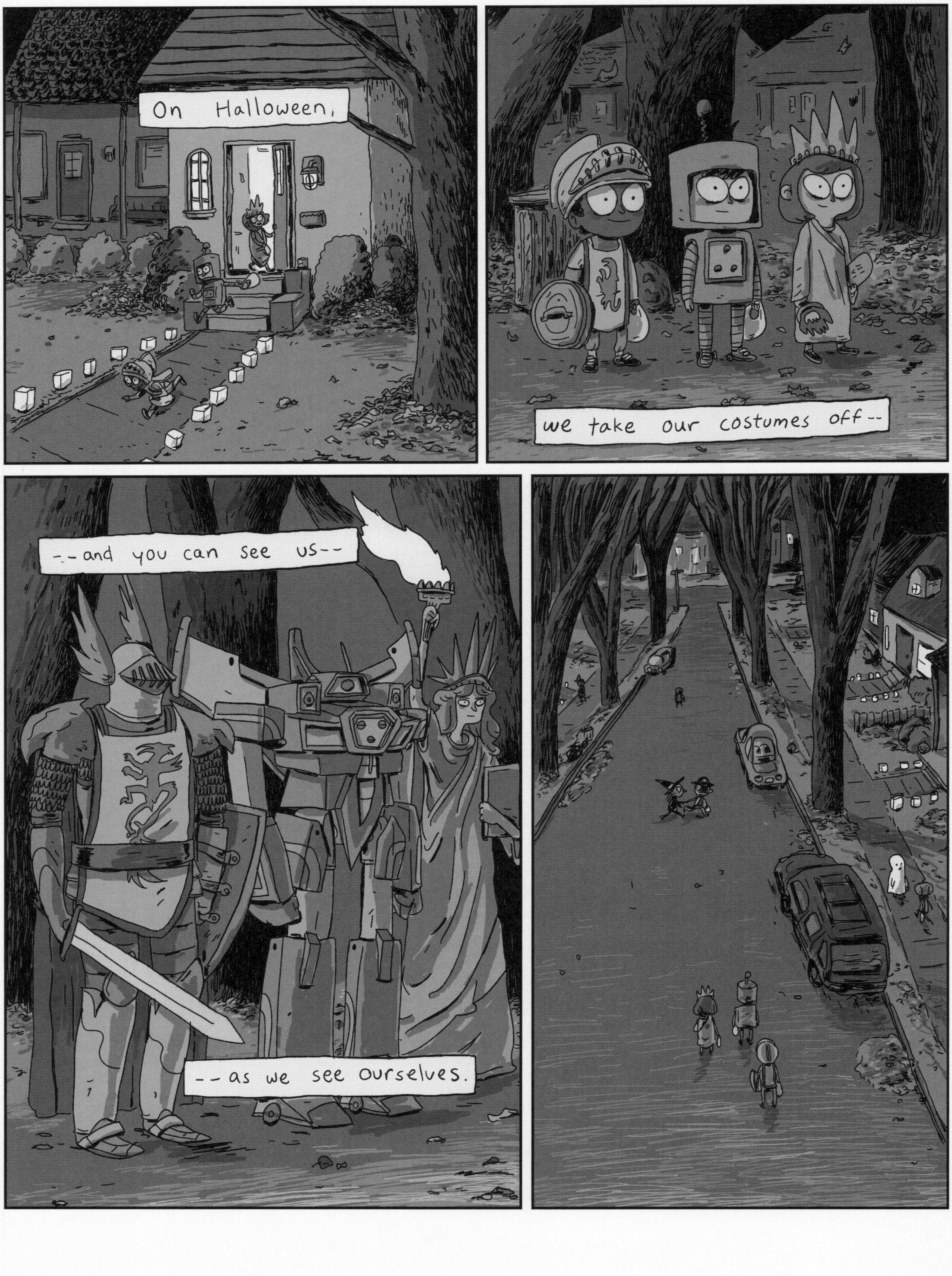
On Halloween,
we take our costumes off--
--and you can see us--
--as we see ourselves.

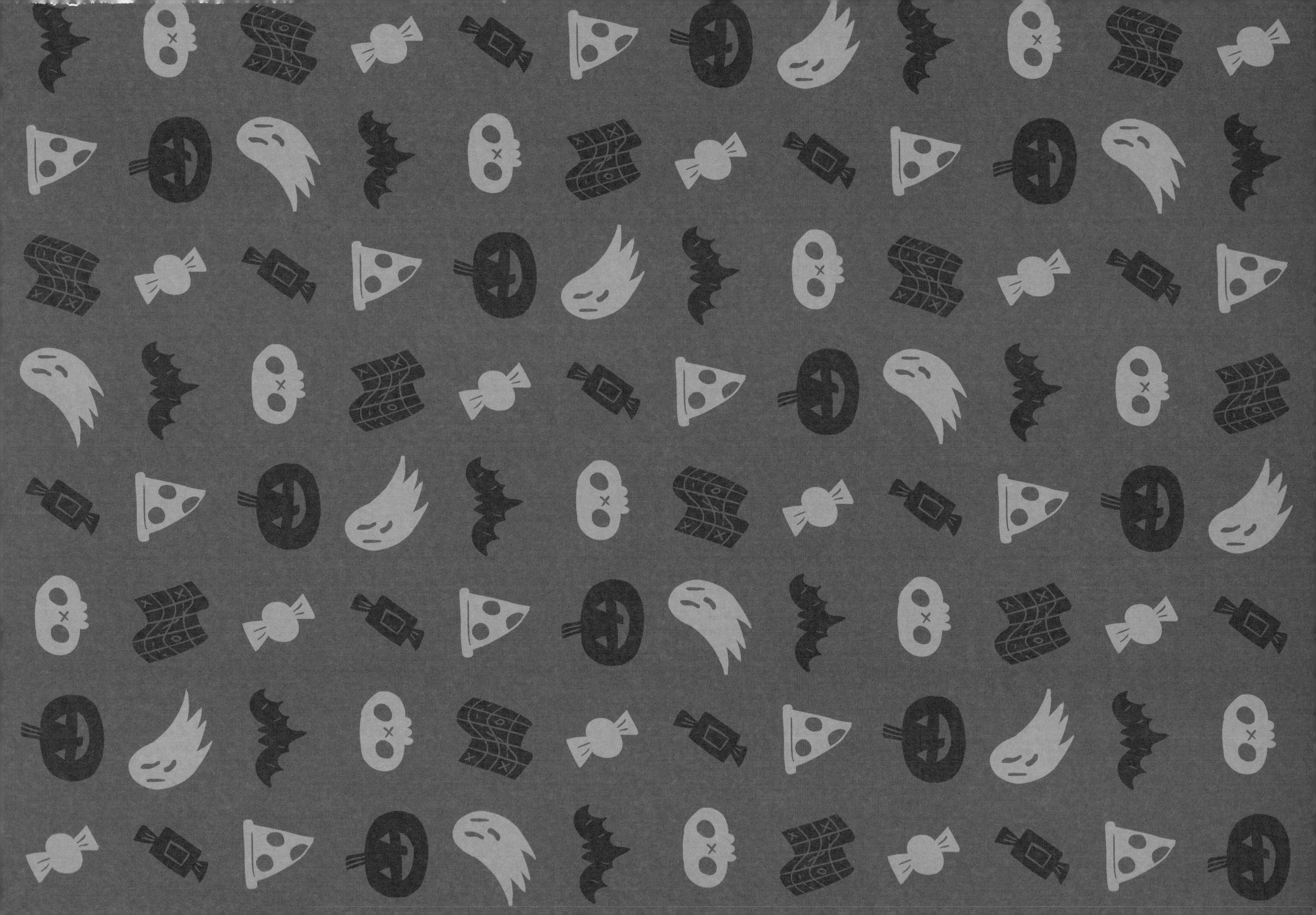